Meet On The Ledge

Fairport Convention – The Classic Years

Also available:

Richard Thompson – Strange Affair

Meet On The Ledge

Fairport Convention – The Classic Years

Patrick Humphries

First published in 1982 by Eel Pie Publishing Ltd
This edition published in 1997 by
Virgin Books
an imprint of Virgin Publishing Ltd
332 Ladbroke Grove
London W10 5AH

Copyright © Patrick Humphries 1982, 1997

ISBN 0 7535 0153 8

Cover picture courtesy of Ashley Hutchings

The right of Patrick Humphries to be identified as the author of this work has been asserted by him in accordance with the Copyright, Designs and Patents Act 1988

This book is sold subject to the condition that it shall not, by way of trade or otherwise, be lent, resold, hired out or circulated without the publisher's prior written consent in any form of binding or cover other than that in which it is published and without a similar condition, including this condition, being imposed upon the subsequent purchaser.

Typeset by TW Typesetting, Plymouth, Devon

Printed and bound in Great Britain by
Mackays of Chatham PLC, Chatham, Kent.

Contents

	The Prologue	**vii**
	Introduction	**xi**
1	Muswell Hillbillies	**1**
2	She Moves Through The Fair	**16**
3	How Dreadful is this Place	**30**
4	Trad. Arr. Fairport	**43**
5	Come All Ye	**53**
6	Walk Awhile	**61**
7	There's a Hole in the Wall . . .	**82**
8	Knights of the Road	**91**
9	Fiddlestix	**105**
10	Farewell, Farewell	**119**
11	Country Pie	**135**
12	Postscript	**140**
	Epilogue, March 1997	**145**
	Discography	**164**
	Cropredy Circles	**171**
	List of Illustrations	**172**

The Prologue

This is the first book that I ever wrote. It was originally commissioned by my good friend Peter Hogan for Pete Townshend's Eel Pie Publishing some time in the late 1970s. Since it was first published in 1982, *Meet On The Ledge* has taken on a life of its own. This is largely due to the perennial appeal of the group that it's about. In the words of the wise, and widely loved, Cropredy host Johnny Jones:

> 'Ladies and gentlemen, the greatest folk-rock band in the world – Fairport Convention!'

The original idea for the book, as I recall, was for a volume telling the story of the British folk revival. We soon realised that a project that ambitious could never be accommodated in anything smaller than the capital city's residential telephone directory. And besides, almost everyone of note in the folk revival had, at one time or another, been involved with Fairport, so voilà – *Meet On The Ledge: A History of Fairport Convention*.

Fairport had been going a mere 15 years by the time *Meet On The Ledge* first appeared, but they were already getting quite good at it. At that time it was still rare to find a rock book about anyone other than Elvis, Dylan or The Beatles, and the reviews were gratifying. It was clear though that this was not so much a testament to the

Meet On The Ledge

quality of my prose as to the high esteem and great affection in which the band were held.

After Eel Pie was taken over, *Meet On The Ledge* disappeared from the shelves, though over the years people continued to produce battered originals for me to sign. I had heard that second-hand copies were swapping hands for up to £40, but was still surprised when someone came up to me at Cropredy '96 and said, rather pointedly, that such prices must be making me a very rich man. At that point I had two copies left, one of which I have just sacrificed to produce this reprint!

I found myself revisiting a lot of the familiar Fairport territory in 1995 when I was writing my biography of Richard Thompson (*Strange Affair*, Virgin, £12.99). It was strange and rather disorientating to look afresh at the Fairport story, and in the first part of *Strange Affair* I wrote again about the early days of Fairport – though inevitably a different take this time around. Perhaps the best comment on the group's origins came from Richard's mum Joan: 'I remember Ashley Hutchings coming to the front door,' she told me conspiratorially, like the woman who had just spotted the monster for the first time in a Hammer horror, 'and that was the first sign of Fairport Convention.'

Simon Nicol's childhood home in North London is now officially part of London's rock'n'roll history. But, as the late Samuel Goldwyn so touchingly observed: 'We've all passed a lot of water since then.' Fairport Convention may never again produce an album as seismic as *Liege & Lief*, but that is as much to do with the musical climate as with Fairport themselves. Besides, if you've made one album which could legitimately be thought to have switched the whole direction of popular music, you might well feel entitled to rest on your laurels. Fairport's appeal isn't simply nostalgia, although that is undeniably a part of it. Fairport just won't go away. In part at least it was

The Prologue

their continuing determination not to quit which made me finally accept the need for this reissue.

Any tattered reputation I have is due to this book. I am terribly fond of it. Of course there are things I'd change here now, but then there are probably things Fairport aren't that happy with on their first album.

Meet On The Ledge is being made available by those awfully nice people at Virgin Publishing more or less as it was back then. I was reluctant to completely rewrite the book because I firmly believe that whatever merit there is in *Meet On The Ledge* comes from its contemporary spin. It was written by a young, first-time author, at a time when Fairport Convention were still very much a working band, and Cropredy village was still best known as the site of a 17th-century Civil War battle. The temptation to go back in, to nip and tuck, to remix, remake and remodel was strong, but in correcting and polishing it would be all too easy to destroy whatever appeal there is in this book. And hell, I can live with the embarrassment of being the right side of 30 again!

When *Meet On The Ledge* first appeared, the future of rock 'n' roll – so the *NME* reliably informed us – lay in the hands of Spandau Ballet. This was a time before *Q* or *Mojo*, long before fanzines; pre-MTV and lavish box sets celebrating Sandy Denny or Richard Thompson. There was no choice but to go to source material for the information I needed. Even then some of the memories were a bit wonky, some of the interviews contradicted each other, but that's part and parcel of oral history. It's a story passed down through the generations. Call it the folk tradition.

Meet On The Ledge finishes as Fairport split in 1979. Although over the intervening years new information has gradually surfaced on Fairport's early history, much of this found its way into the first part of *Strange Affair*. Besides, to look back from the mid-90s, and try to rewrite

Meet On The Ledge

a book largely about the 1960s, actually written in the late 1970s, struck me as a short cut to Breakdown Central.

What I hope you will find in the following pages is a certain period charm and a quaint telling of a tale in hard, and soft, times. The tale of Fairport Convention, and the way we were.

Patrick Humphries
London, March 1997

Introduction

A history of Fairport Convention can never be that simple. A band with more playing changes than the England cricket team; a band whose influence spread far beyond 'folk'. Their story must, invariably, touch on their influences, their influence, and the times they were part of.

Fairport surfaced during the heady London underground of the late sixties, and disbanded in the post-Punk summer of 1979. They were a group which was, somehow, greater than its parts – a fine foundation for the nurturing of individual talents like Sandy Denny, Richard Thompson, Ashley Hutchings and Ian Matthews. But Fairport were in themselves a great band. Frequently their internal frictions became publicly apparent, and were reflected in the shoddiness of certain albums. But when the magic crackled, there wasn't a band in the land to touch them.

They will be best remembered as the instigators of 'folk/rock', 'electric folk' or whatever it's called now. Fairport ignored the traditional toes on which they trod. They made a wide, young audience aware of the 'folk tradition'. Even if only a small percentage of that audience bothered to trace a 'Trad. Arr. Fairport' song back – either to its roots (the Copper Family, Walter Pardon) or one of the more academic revivalists (Martin Carthy, Peter Bellamy) – that in itself was an achievement. Fairport may only have scratched the surface as far as the folk tradition went, but they sowed the seeds for the fertile harvest which was to follow. Bands like Steeleye Span, Five Hand Reel and the Home Service took their cue from Fairport.

A Fairport hallmark was their diversity, which meant they could incorporate rock 'n' roll, country, blues, cajun, bluegrass, almost anything they turned their hand to. (Their canon of Dylan songs was, in itself, sufficient proof of their interpretive ability.)

It is ironic that a band as influential as Fairport never realised their proper commercial potential. They were capable of filling concert halls across the world, and their albums were steady sellers. But they never achieved the financial or managerial stability which would, surely, have given their music a boost. As Bob Woffinden so pertinently noted in the *NME Encyclopedia Of Rock*: 'It would be difficult to name a band that's paid more dues and been rewarded with such wretched luck!'

Fairport coiled through the late sixties and seventies like an errant snail, and in tracing their history I have tried to be as objective as possible. I have relied on quotes to illustrate points, rather than my own interpretation and opinion. Obviously, opinions on certain albums and events will differ, and if I have strayed from the path of impartiality, it is in the direction of Richard Thompson. His music, both with Fairport and since, has, I feel, been the most satisfying and durable.

Fairport were a band for all seasons, whether it was the rock 'n' rolling revelry of a live show, with Swarb and Richard pushing each other to the limit, or the intimacy of a revolving record, with the comforting words 'Fairport Convention' stamped on the pink label. In the end, those records provide the permanent proof, and I hope this book sheds some light on the people responsible for those records.

This all sounds terribly pompous. I love Fairport, warts and all. I love the music they created, and the effect it had

Introduction

on me. I'll never forget the kindness of Dave Pegg, Richard Thompson and Sandy, the only time I ever met her. I'm willing to forget the duff gigs and albums if they are. Fairport have provided some of the best musical memories I'm likely to have, and that's the reason I wrote this book. At their best, they *were* the best. Even now, they manage to avoid the cosy safety of nostalgia – the 1981 shows proved they were willing to re-visit that foreign country which is called the past, and add something fresh to it.

A great many people helped me with this book. I'm only sorry that my mum wasn't alive to see it published, and see some of the faith she always had in me repaid. But wherever you are now, this is for you, Paddy.

I would particularly like to thank Philippa Clare-Wood, whose initial co-operation was invaluable. Nigel Cross, John Tobler, Pete Frame, Janet Funamoto, Kingsley Abbott, Brian Wyvill, Edward Haber, Neil Storey, Fiona Taylor, Neil Raphael, Helen Cinnamon, Hugh Price, John Platt, Chris Groom and Karl Dallas kindly lent me their time, cuttings and memories.

Many thanks for the help and sound counsel to Pete Hogan, Robert Shelton, Ian Dawnay, Susy Park, Bill Brooke, Bob Woffinden, Simon Nicol, Richard and Linda Thompson, Ashley Hutchings, Joe Boyd, Anthea Joseph, Dave Mattacks, Martin Satterthwaite, Mike Sparrow, P1/003, Jo Lustig, Bernard Doherty, Robin Lamble, Colin Irwin and, of course, all and any who were part of it!

1 Muswell Hillbillies

To begin somewhere near the beginning, amongst the pages of the *Finchley Press* of 29 September, 1967. Buried inauspiciously at the bottom of page three – between an account of the Finchley Horticultural Society's 27th Annual Show, and the gravedigger who broke down in the dock sobbing: 'I just could not stand digging graves any longer!' – was the tantalising headline: 'Their First Record!' The paragraph ran: 'A Muswell Hill pop group, the Fairport Convention, who got their name from Fairport House, Fortis Green, where they rehearse, went to a recording studio last week to make their first record. The group is comprised of four entertainers, two of which come from Fortis Green – Simon Nichol [sic] and Tyger Hutchins [sic] – and one from Whetstone, Richard Thompson.'

Well, it was that sort of summer. There was nothing unusual about a 'pop group' calling itself 'Fairport Convention' – percolating across the Atlantic that year were such extraordinarily named ensembles as Country Joe and the Fish, Jefferson Airplane and the Grateful Dead. The languid vibes emanating from San Francisco that summer even managed to make it up the 43 bus route to safe, stolid Muswell Hill (later immortalised by Ray Davies of the Kinks on *Muswell Hillbillies*).

It was the best of trips, the worst of trips. The scene had switched from the crass commercialism of 'Swinging

Meet On The Ledge

London' to the enthusiastic alternatives of San Francisco. The London underground was taking its cue from the Haight, clubs and bands were springing up quicker than kaftan manufacturers, and *Sergeant Pepper*'s acid-obsessed, music hall mysticism had affected everyone with an ounce of hip. *The Times* consulted A. Pope on the legalisation of cannabis, Day-Glo posters adorned the capital, the Pink Floyd played lengthy sets to a surreal backdrop of ectoplasmic light shows. Procol Harum tripped the light fantastic with 'Whiter Shade Of Pale', and a splendid time was guaranteed for all!

Folk music was locked deep in dusty vaults beneath Cecil Sharp House. Rock 'n' roll lay emasculated behind the daunting walls of Graceland, the home of Elvis (in Ian Dury's immortal phrase – 'The Duke of Windsor of rock 'n' roll'). Dylan's electric odyssey had ended up mangled on a country road, and no word came from his Woodstock eyrie. The Beatles followed *Pepper* with that summer's anthem – 'All You Need Is Love'. The pirate radio stations were blasting out an invigorating diet of West Coast psychedelia, and in the burgeoning London clubs you could see the home-grown variety: The Who, Jimi Hendrix, Procol Harum, Cream, Pink Floyd, all at their peak of musical innovation.

The generation reared on Elvis and the Everlys, affected by the Beatles and given voice by Dylan, were caught up in the enthusiasm prevalent that summer. Genuine alternatives to the strictures of a shallow society suddenly seemed possible, particularly with the facilities and outlets available. It was into this florid maelstrom that 'pop group' Fairport Convention plunged.

The genesis of Fairport Convention can be traced back to a fluid band Ashley 'Tyger' Hutchings was involved with during the early sixties, the name changing as frequently as the personnel: the Still Waters, the Blues Reeds, Dr K's Blues Band, Tim Turner's Narration (named after the guy who used to narrate *Look At Life*), the Electric Dysentry and, penultimately, the Ethnic Shuffle Orchestra. As one-time manager, bass player and musical director of those early bands, Ashley Hutchings is a good thread to follow in the Gordian Knot which constitutes the history of Fairport Convention.

He was born in January 1945, and lived around North London for the majority of his early life. His father was a self-taught musician, a pianist with his own dance band – Leonard Hutchings And His Embassy Five. Ashley was an early rock 'n' roll casualty, listening to Elvis and Bill Haley on Radio Luxembourg every night, always buying the original American versions rather than the ersatz English covers. That habit of tracing material back to source is a trait which stayed with him throughout his musical career; he never settled for second best.

The only indigenous music that Hutchings had a real fondness for at that time was skiffle. As with so many of his generation, Lonnie Donegan exercised a strong influence on the young Hutchings.

Skiffle was a do-it-yourself sort of music and young Ashley was the proud possessor of a tea-chest bass. 'I bought a bass guitar when I was 16, and have stuck with that ever since.'*

His early quest for musical knowledge he called 'exhaustive ... My week might very often be taken up with six nights out, and each night a different musical form ... Jazz clubs, folk clubs, classical concerts, rock clubs, like the Ferry Inn, the Flamingo, the Marquee.'

Hutchings' early working life was spent as a journalist with magazines like *Furnishing World* and *Advertising Weekly*, a brief spell in an export house, then as an assistant to the managing director of Haymarket Press. It was during that time that 'it suddenly dawned on me that I could actually try and make a living out of music'.

*Unless otherwise stated, all quotations are from interviews conducted by the author.

Meet On The Ledge

The North Bank Youth Club in Muswell Hill (where the Kinks first started out as the Ravens) gave Hutchings a stage for his various groups, and it was there that a rudimentary Fairport line-up began to take shape with the Ethnic Shuffle mob: Ashley on stand-up bass and Simon Nicol on guitar.

Simon John Breckenridge Nicol was born in October 1950, the youngest in a family of four. His father was a doctor practising in Fortis Green, and his surgery was the family home – Fairport. Simon left Friern Barnet School at 15 and worked as a projectionist at the Highgate Odeon for six months. In 1961 he acquired his first guitar, and he was a regular visitor to the North Bank Club, where he watched the procession of Ashley's bands passing through.

Simon: 'Ashley was always the mastermind behind these various outfits, which were – in the main – urban R&B bands, but even then he was prone to come up with more obscure material than that which was in circulation . . . He was always a bit of an *éminence grise*, so the first time he asked me in (to the Ethnic Shuffle), I was a little bit chuffed.' Nicol remembers the Ethnic Shuffle Orchestra as 'a C&W jug band, transmogrified into the Lovin' Spoonful. By the time we started doing the Byrds stuff, the washboards had been put away!'

Due to a complicated lease his father left when he died in 1964, Simon and his mother had to move to a flat 50 yards up the road, and were forced to rent 'Fairport' out. The house was divided into bedsits for transient students, nurses . . . and one Ashley Hutchings, who used the large rooms as rehearsal areas for his various musical ensembles. Nicol left the Odeon job, as the band was taking up too much time, and his mother supported him as a musician: 'which was wonderful of her, because the only gigs we were doing were friends' weddings and barmitzvahs, at £10 a time'.

The as yet unnamed 'Fairport Convention' began to

take recognisable shape with the addition of guitarist Richard Thompson, from Totteridge. Simon: 'Brian Wyvill, who was a friend of mine, lived two doors away from Tyger (in Durnsford Road, where another close neighbour was Prof. Bruce Lacey) and was at school with Richard, and used to go on about his wizard friend, who was just as good a guitarist as Hank Marvin.'

Richard Thompson was born in April 1949, the son of a policeman, and spent his early life around North London, with frequent holidays to Scotland, where his father came from. He attended William Ellis School near Parliament Hill Fields, where his contemporaries included Gerry Conway (later of Fotheringay and Jethro Tull) and Hugh Cornwell (later of the Stranglers and Her Majesty's Pleasure). Brian Wyvill remembers the young Thompson as 'a master train spotter', and for his radical reworking of Dylan's 'Mr Tambourine Man' as 'Mr Margarine Man', and his note-for-note version of the Shadows' 'Foot-Tapper'.

Thompson went through the obligatory school bands, the Rotations and Emil And The Detectives, with Thompson on guitar (a Hofner V3 with – for some obscure reason – the medieval English word 'Falan' on it), Hugh Cornwell on bass and Nick Jones (son of *Melody Maker*'s redoubtable Max Jones, and himself a writer for *MM* in later years) on drums. Their repertoire consisted mainly of regurgitated Buddy Holly and Everly Brothers songs.

Thompson learnt guitar from friends of his elder sister (the most influential of whom, Big Muldoon, later received a dedication on the sleeve of Thompson's first solo album in 1972). On leaving school, he became apprenticed to a stained-glass window maker, Hans Unger, for six months (an example of his craft can still be seen in St Columbus Church in Chester). In an interview published much later, Thompson recalled his days there: 'I was a funky sort of Clapton follower, but in the studio they'd have the Third Programme on all the time. I became really interested in classical music, and much of my guitar style comes from people like Debussy – which is by no means as outlandish as it sounds.'

Simon remembers Richard turning up as a dep for a session, 'but after he came there were no more guitarists. Number one in a field of one', and Nicol happily settled down as rhythm guitarist. It was mainly Ashley who decided upon the group's musical input. Richard remembered Ashley thus: 'When I first met him, Tyger thought he was Frankie Avalon, with his flashy socks and sneakers!'

It was Richard Lewis, a friend of Simon's and an 'amateur musicologist' (with an extensive record collection which Simon and Ashley frequently plundered in search of material) who suggested the name 'Fairport Convention', and it was under that name that the band made their debut, at St Michael's Church Hall, Golders Green, which had been booked for the princely sum of £5. The gig was on the same day that *Sergeant Pepper* and *Are You Experienced* were released.

The four of them – Richard and Simon on guitars, Ashley on bass and Shawn Frater on drums (his only gig with Fairport under their new name, although he had drummed with the Ethnic Shuffle Orchestra) – played to a less than capacity audience a set that included Love's 'Seven And Seven Is', 'Hey Joe', and Dylan's 'My Back Pages'. Amongst those in the audience were Kingsley Abbott and his friend Martin Lamble, both from University College School. Simon: 'At the end of that gig, this chap came up to us in a parka – his Lambretta was parked outside – and announced himself to be one Martin Lamble of Harrow, which was a place beyond our ken.' Lamble said he thought he was a better drummer than Frater. Taking him on his word the band asked him round to audition the following week – which he duly did, landing the gig as Fairport Convention's new drummer.

1 Muswell Hillbillies

Martin Francis Lamble was born in August 1949 in St John's Wood. His playing experience was limited to a couple of UCS bands – Captain Rugeley's Blues Band and the enigmatic Pheg. His younger brother Robin (who played bass in Al Stewart's band Shot In The Dark) felt that had Martin not joined Fairport, he would quite happily have taken a career as a railway signalman, as it combined both his fascinations – model railways and technical drawing.

Neil Raphael, who was also at school with Martin at UCS, felt he was a very mature drummer for his age: 'As someone who hadn't played drums for long, he did a lot of extemporising . . . I think he would have been a fine drummer, he had sensibility on his head.'

Fairport made £10 profit on their first gig, and blew it all immediately afterwards on a Chinese meal. Those very early Fairport gigs consisted almost wholly of songs by American acts, which the band extracted from the extensive record collections of Kingsley Abbott, and brothers Danny and Richard Lewis. That American bias was to cause some confusion for the band later on. Ashley: 'We were quite derivative, but our sources were pretty obscure compared with those days.' Among songs featured at those early gigs were the late Richard Farina's 'Reno, Nevada' and 'The Bold Marauder' ('Farina was a great influence,' recalled Ashley), Dylan's 'Lay Down Your Weary Tune' and 'Chimes Of Freedom', Phil Ochs' 'Flower Lady', Buddy Guy's 'Messin' With The Man', the Airplane's 'Plastic Fantastic Lover', Paul Butterfield's 'East/West' and Dino Valenti's 'Get Together'.

However, a singer was needed. Thompson suffered a slight speech impediment, which, coupled with his natural reticence, made him very subdued on stage. Simon was the front man, introducing the songs, and Ashley had little real confidence in his own singing. Other voices were needed to swell the Fairport ranks.

Meet On The Ledge

The first to arrive was an eighteen-year-old willowy blonde librarian, Judy Aileen Dyble, who lived in the same corner of North London. She had first sung with a group, Judy And The Folkmen, whose first gig had been in the daunting confines of the Hornsey Conservative Association in 1964!

In a *Zig Zag* interview in 1970, she recalled how she had been asked to join Fairport: 'I was sitting in Alexandra Palace one evening, when a little man called Tyger Hutchings came along, and I told him I didn't like Eric Clapton. And he said, "Oh really? You're mad, would you like to join a group?"'

Fairport did a number of gigs as a five piece, but it became apparent that they were still light in the vocal department, so Ashley began ringing round to try and find a male singer. Ian Matthews (Macdonald) was born in June 1946, a Scunthorpe lad who had been apprenticed to Bradford Football Club and played in a couple of local Lincolnshire bands, the Classics and the Rebels, before moving south to Swinging London to seek fame and fortune. He ended up working in Ravel's shoe shop in Carnaby Street. Matthews was a singer with what John Tobler called 'the first (only?) English surfing band' – Pyramid. They had a couple of singles issued on Deram, and were managed for a time by Procol Harum's manager, but never scored a hit. Pyramid's lead singer Steve Hyatt was sitting in Tony Hall's office at Deram when Ashley Hutchings rang to say he was looking for a singer for Fairport. Hall passed the message on to Hyatt, who suggested Matthews.

With an augmented line up, the six-piece Fairport Convention went out gigging round the underground haunts during the late summer and early autumn of 1967. Their gigs were booked by a friend, John Penhallow, who was acting as the band's manager. Simon: 'All through that summer we were playing gigs, mainly all-night efforts. Richard would rattle about in the van afterwards, then turn up at the stained glass place. He was always slicing his hand on razor-sharp edges of glass because he was so tired.'

Fairport were very much a part of the London underground circuit. (Richard: 'I think, basically, the underground embraced anyone that wasn't doing Otis Redding riffs!') They were strange bedfellows to Mick Farren's Social Deviants, the Soft Machine and Family at all the familiar haunts like Happening 44, Middle Earth, the Electric Garden and UFO. They did, though, manage to land a prestige gig supporting Procol Harum at Brian Epstein's Saville Theatre.

It was Tommy Vance who coined the 'English Jefferson Airplane' tag. Simon: 'Maybe it was the way the name scanned ... there's something about the name "Fairport Convention" which suggested America. We got introduced a couple of times as "All the way from Hollywood, USA", and we thought "Whaaat?"' The similarities also extended to the fact that both bands had female singers as their focal points, and of course Fairport's repertoire was still drawn extensively from America.

John Penhallow managed to land the band a gig at the infamous UFO club, where American whizz kid Joe Boyd was ostensibly 'musical director'. Boyd, then only 24, was from Boston, and had managed to cram an awful lot into his 24 summers. He had been production manager at the traumatic 1965 Newport Festival, when Dylan had astounded the folk world by blasting out folk-rock with the Paul Butterfield Blues Band (who had been discovered by Boyd in Chicago, and signed by Paul Rothchild to Elektra). As a reward, Boyd ran the Elektra offices in London for a year, where he helped produce the 1966 album *What's Shakin'*, which featured Eric Clapton and Steve Winwood among its participants. During the winter of 1966, he had helped, along with John Hopkins, to establish the UFO club in London's Tottenham Court Road. Apart from managing the Incredible String Band, Boyd also produced the first Pink Floyd single 'Arnold Layne', but was dropped by them when EMIs insisted on using a staff producer.

In a *Melody Maker* piece of June 1967, Chris Welch had fearlessly plunged into 'The Underground', and Joe Boyd described UFO to him thus: 'The object of the club is to provide a place for experimental pop music and also for the mixing of the medias, light shows and theatrical happenings.' Membership was 15 shillings a year, and members paid ten bob on the door. Ah, long ago and far away.

Richard remembered Fairport sharing their first UFO gig with the Incredibles and the Pink Floyd ('and thinking they were terrible'). They managed to impress Boyd, who talked about getting them a deal with his Witchseason Company, which he was in the process of setting up. Simon: 'True to his word, we were in a contract signing situation within a couple of weeks.'

Joe Boyd's recollection of when he first saw Fairport differs from theirs, and he cannot recall them playing UFO with the Incredibles or the Floyd. The first time he remembers seeing Fairport Convention was at a strip club in Soho's Gerrard Street that had been transformed, literally overnight, into a 'psychedelic club' – Happening 44. Boyd was favourably impressed, and offered them the 5 a.m. 'New Bands' spot at UFO. Joe: 'The thing about Fairport when I first went down to see them at the strip club ... it wasn't Judy, and it wasn't the band, and it wasn't the music that interested me. It was Richard that interested me from the very beginning – to see this 17-year-old kid playing incredibly mature guitar solos ... Essentially my primary interest in Fairport Convention was in Richard, because he was obviously the most talented.'

It was Boyd who put the band on a wage of £10 a week each (which was later upped to £12.50). Their advance came in the shape of new equipment from Track Records, to whom they signed first, sharing the label with the Who and Jimi Hendrix.

The first Fairport Convention record was a Track single, 'If I Had a Ribbon Bow', which was released in November 1967. It was a 1936 song, first recorded by Maxine Sullivan, which Judy had found while going through Boyd's record collection. Simon remembered the band having a 'terrible time' recording it at Sound Techniques' studio in Chelsea. 'We learnt it, arranged it, and recorded it in four sections, then poor John Wood (who was resident engineer and co-owner of the studio) had to snip it all together on an Ampex 4-track vertical machine.' He was less than enthusiastic about their prospects.

The other side of their debut single was 'If (Stomp)', which was credited to Macdonald/Thompson, and it was a marginally different version of the song from that which appeared on their first album. Ian: 'I didn't have a very big involvement in that song. Richard already had the song, but it wasn't long enough and he needed two more verses. So I just wrote two more verses for him.' From those sessions also came demos of Joni Mitchell's 'Both Sides Now', Eric Andersen's 'Violets Of Dawn', Dylan's 'Lay Down Your Weary Tune', and a different version of Harvey Brooks and Jim Glover's 'One Sure Thing'.

'Ribbon Bow' failed to set the charts on fire, but undaunted, Fairport returned to the studio to begin recording their first album. The first Fairport album on Polydor (Track's parent company, who re-issued it in 1973 with a different cover) is an interesting reflection of their predilection for things West Coast, and redolent of the dreamy late sixties sound. The choice of material is eclectic, drawn from songs which had impressed them in Kingsley Abbott and Richard Lewis's record collections, unreleased Joni Mitchell material, and songs the band themselves were writing.

Simon: 'A lot of good material was learnt in the studio, most of which went into our performing repertoire ... A lot of stuff we were doing on stage wasn't worth recording, because it was too well known ... we had a chance to record some really interesting material.'

The album opens with an Emitt Rhodes song, 'Time Will Show The Wiser'. Rhodes was an American singer/songwriter, and the song comes from his A&M *Merrygoround* album. (It was also the song chosen to illustrate that first Fairport album by Richard Thompson for his 1976 *Guitar, Vocal* anthology.) The two Joni Mitchell songs came via Joe Boyd, who had known her in the States, and had helped her obtain a publishing deal with Essex Music in the UK. She had left a tape of ten or so songs here, which Fairport heard, and decided to include 'I Don't Know Where I Stand' and 'Chelsea Morning'. They were also including versions of her songs 'Marcie' and 'Night In The City' as part of their repertoire at that time. (Kingsley Abbott can remember the band puzzling over exactly what the 'incense owl' mentioned on 'Chelsea Morning' actually was!)

The two songs credited to Ghosh/Horvitch/Thompson – 'Sun Shade', and the wistful 'Decameron' – were written by Richard and two school friends of his, Paul Ghosh and Andy Horvitch. 'The Lobster' has a tune by Ashley and Richard, the words coming from a poem by George Painter. 'One Sure Thing' was from the 1966 Verve album *Changes* by Harvey Brooks and Jim Glover (which also included 'Lay Down Your Weary Tune' and 'Flower Lady' and was where Fairport learnt those songs).

Ian Matthews was credited on the sleeve as playing Jew's Harp, but – as he later recalled in John Tobler's exhaustive *Zig Zag* piece – 'That was the studio thing, they just wanted me to look good, because I didn't play anything else at the time. I did play it on "M1 Breakdown", and I really cut my mouth open too. I went to listen to the playback with blood dripping down my face!'

Dylan's influence is stamped indelibly upon the album, from the punning title of 'It's Alright Ma, It's Only Witchcraft' to what is arguably the album's most interesting track, 'Jack O'Diamonds'. It was not the 1957 Lonnie Donegan hit, but a curious amalgam: the words were extracted from the poems on the sleeve of Dylan's fourth album, *Another Side Of*... which had been set to music by American actor Ben Carruthers. It was issued as a single by Ben Carruthers and the Deep on Parlophone in 1965, and was also featured on the BBC Play For Today, *Man Without Papers*, in which Carruthers acted. Legend has it that it came to Fairport's attention when Richard Thompson played the single to Ashley and suggested they record it. Ashley is 'almost convinced' that it was Hugh Cornwell who lent the single to Richard in the first place.

Ian wanted Richard to take the lead vocal on the record, as he did on stage. But Thompson's stubborn reticence ensured it was Matthews who eventually sang on it. Live, Fairport would play the song out with Simon Nicol on fiddle on a tune called 'Spanish Lady', which they'd nicked from an old John Handy album. Harnessing all the technology available, Fairport electrified the fiddle by strapping an old telephone pick-up to it!

Compared to the excesses perpetrated in the name of 'progressive' music in those days, Fairport's first album shows considerable restraint and retains its charm today. The strengths of the album lie in the effective blending of Ian and Judy's voices (notably on 'Chelsea Morning') and the odd surge of Thompson's already unique guitar style in evidence on 'It's Alright Ma . . .'. The playing is pretty subdued throughout, although both Hutchings' bass and Lamble's drumming are strongly evident. The faults lie in Joe Boyd's flat and uninspired production (perhaps because one is more used to his later, exemplary work), and in Judy Dyble's listless and remote singing, particularly on the beautiful 'One Sure Thing'.

Meet On The Ledge

The initial reviews were encouraging, if not overly enthusiastic. A Polydor advertisement at the time called the album: 'One put together by unusual personalities for that insignificant minority of seekers to whom real music, oddly enough, seems to matter.'

It was not long after the release of the album that the first split occurred in the Fairport ranks. It was a situation which became almost synonymous with the band, and which dogged them throughout their 12-year career. Judy Dyble was asked to leave, for a number of reasons. Ian: 'I think it became a bit strained between her and everyone – it was increasingly clear that she really wasn't going to make it as a singer in that band... she had a tendency to sing sharp. I don't think I know any other singer that has that tendency.' Ashley: 'It was very difficult, and very sad. I think the band was getting stronger, heavier, and Judy's voice – which had always been light – was suffering because of it. When we started we were quite a light band and played acoustic guitars on occasions, but after Ian joined, we were getting heavier.' Simon remembered her as being 'very shy, hiding behind her glasses'.

So Judy left, and went on to join the nascent King Crimson, in the shape of Giles, Giles and Fripp, for one month, recording briefly with them. (Her version of Crimson's 'I Talk To The Wind' appears on the compilation *A Young Person's Guide To King Crimson*.) She then joined up with ex-Them keyboardist Jackie MacAuley to form Trader Horn, who recorded one album for Dawn. Little has been heard of her since then, although she was involved in trying to get a deal with Pye as a solo singer.

The five-man line-up played about half a dozen gigs without Judy, but because of the 'English Jefferson Airplane' tag, they had acquired a reputation for featuring a female singer. Simon: 'We felt it could be okay, but everybody who came to see us wanted to know where the girl was. We hadn't realised just how much of an impression she had created, and we didn't want to go cap in hand to Judy . . .'

So the band held auditions in the inauspicious surroundings of the Eight Feathers Boys Club in Fulham. ('Only one thing worse than going for an audition', recalled Simon, 'and that's holding one.') From the ten or so girls they auditioned, one emerged head and shoulders above the competition – Sandy Denny. Linda Thompson remembered Sandy telling her about her audition for Fairport: 'She had already established quite a reputation in the folk clubs, so when Fairport said, "What are you going to sing?" Sandy said, "Well, I'd like you to play something for me first!"' (Before the audition, like many other people, Sandy thought Fairport were an American group.)

Simon: 'She stood out like a clean glass in a sinkful of dirty dishes . . . it was a one-horse race, really. The only question was, "Was she too shy or nervous to settle in?" ' Fortunately for all concerned, she was not. But Joe Boyd, who was in the States at the time, had his doubts: 'I got a call that Judy was going to leave, and that they had been having some talks with Sandy Denny about joining. I was a little alarmed, because I felt she was temperamentally very, very different from them, and I didn't know how it would work out. But I was impressed that they had gone and talked with her and felt it was a good sign, because they were – at that time – very shy and diffident people, and Sandy was, to say the least, a very extrovert, strong personality. I was afraid she might dominate the band, but I think I underestimated the stubbornness of Richard and Ashley.'

With Sandy in the band, Fairport Convention prepared to enter their halcyon period, the one for which they are best remembered.

2 She Moves Through The Fair

Alexandra Elene Maclean Denny was born in Wimbledon on 6 January 1947. She left school armed with two 'A' levels, and went on to Kingston Art College, where her contemporaries included John Renbourn, Jimmy Page and Eric Clapton. Uncertain of exactly what to do, she worked as a nurse at the Brompton Chest Hospital. In the evenings she was working the folk clubs as a solo performer, and going steady with the American singer/songwriter Jackson C. Frank, who wrote the oft-covered 'Blues Run The Game'. Sandy first sang in public at the Barge in Kingston-Upon-Thames, then trudged round the folk circuit of the Scots Hoose, Cousins and Bunjies, armed only with her guitar and a voice of startling purity. Her repertoire in those early days was heavily American influenced, consisting of songs by Tom Paxton and, naturally, Jackson C. Frank, plus the occasional folk song. A selection of her material from those days is available on the Mooncrest album *The Original Sandy Denny*, recorded in 1967 and re-issued in 1978.

Sandy joined the Strawbs for six months in 1968, and recorded one album with them. Dave Cousins remembered her doing a floor spot at the Troubadour 'looking like an angel, and singing like one'. The album was recorded on a 2-track machine in Sweden, but was not officially released here until 1973 on a budget label. *All Our Own Work* by Sandy Denny and the Strawbs is

2 She Moves Through The Fair

virtually a showcase for the material of their leader and principal songwriter Dave Cousins, and contains a number of his excellent songs beautifully sung by Sandy. It was a foretaste of what was to come on the splendid 'proper' Strawbs debut album on A&M the following year.

The album is of interest for its inclusion of what is probably still Sandy's best-known song – 'Who Knows Where The Time Goes'. Marginally slower and looser than the version which appeared on *Unhalfbricking*, with only an acoustic guitar backing, the opening line on this 1968 recording is 'Across the *purple* sky . . .', differing slightly from the later version. It is the only Sandy Denny composition on the album, but she is in fine voice throughout.

Cousins recalls that first album as one of 'considerable charm', and felt that, perhaps, Sandy and the Strawbs might well have become Britain's answer to the Mamas and Papas, but it was not to be. They went their separate ways – Sandy back to the clubs as a solo performer, and the Strawbs on to Rick Wakeman and beyond!

Sandy's joining Fairport suddenly made available a whole new strand of material, that of traditional English folk, although that would not become apparent until later. A cassette of the band made around that time (possibly as a demo tape for Island) – assembled surreptitiously by Ashley Hutchings, and not made available until some years later, under the title of *Heyday* – demonstrated that Fairport were still under the sway of their initial American influences. Included are songs by the Everly Brothers ('Gone Gone, Gone' and 'Some Sweet Day'), Richard Farina ('Reno, Nevada') and Leonard Cohen ('Bird On The Wire' and 'Suzanne', a mighty version of the latter – a highlight of many a Fairport set – which demonstrates the wisdom of employing two lead singers, and also the excellence of Martin Lamble as a drummer; his sombre rolls enhance the song considerably). Also included is a version of 'Meet On The Ledge' from a BBC session in

Meet On The Ledge

late 1968. Raunchier and fuller than the 'official' version issued later, the chorus is swelled by such Fairport stalwarts as Kingsley Abbott, Paul Ghosh and Andy Horvitch.

Joe Boyd had moved his catalogue of artists on the Witchseason roster to Island Records while Fairport were in the process of mixing their second album for Polydor. Island was, at the time, England's premier 'progressive' label, featuring Jethro Tull, John Martyn, Traffic and the tragically underrated Nick Drake, among others. So it was that Fairport's second album was scheduled for release on Island, and the label became irrevocably associated with the band until their departure in 1977.

1968 saw Fairport gigging extensively, and also doing a great many BBC radio broadcasts, some tapes of which still exist. An article in the August 1968 issue of *Beat Instrumental* (titled 'Britain's New Breed' – the photo caption for which called Fairport a 'shattering live experience', which was also the title of a Simon Nicol track on the *Heyday* cassette) was already calling Thompson 'one of the best lead guitarists in the country ... whose sleepy-looking face belies the complexity and inventiveness of his work'. In an interview in the same magazine, published in November 1968, Thompson spoke of his dissatisfaction with Fairport's first album and the 'Ribbon Bow' single. Similarities between Fairport and the West Coast bands were also raised, to which Thompson replied: 'There are similarities ... but there's one big and basic difference. They all seem to be doing a sort of cross between rock and soul – look at Big Brother, Country Joe and Jefferson Airplane – it's not all that far from the sock-it-to-me thing, and very American. We think of ourselves as a folk-based band. This is even more pronounced now that Sandy Denny is with us ... She really knows what the folk tradition is all about, and the group as a whole are drawing from the English roots. The fact that we're electric doesn't make any difference.'

2 She Moves Through The Fair

That year, fans also had the opportunity to judge how the 'English Jefferson Airplane' tag stood up in the cold light of day. Well, on a rainy September evening actually, when Fairport appeared with the Airplane at a free concert in Parliament Hill Fields, a couple of days before the Airplane appeared with the Doors at the Roundhouse. Before an audience estimated at barely more than 150, Fairport acquitted themselves admirably (despite the late arrival of Sandy), and displayed how American-influenced they still were.

The band was almost spoilt for choice when it came to selecting material for their second album. Ashley: 'There was a lot of good material around, which became increasingly more available to us. The guys were writing and Sandy was bringing material in, so that there was a lot of competition for the material on that album to be good ... I remember very clearly that the turnover of material around that period was incredible ... A whole bag of things were never recorded.' Among these were Johnny Cash's 'I Still Miss Someone', Gene Clarke's 'Tried So Hard', Eric Andersen's 'Close The Door Lightly When You Go', Tim Buckley's 'Morning Glory' and songs by Richie Havens and Tim Hardin. Coupled with the emergence of Sandy Denny and Richard Thompson as writers of unique and individual substance, plus Sandy's infusion of traditional material, Fairport had few worries as far as new material was concerned. Of Thompson's writing at that time, Joe Boyd had the feeling that: 'He was writing a lot more than anyone knew, but he wasn't showing it to people. But when he did come in with a song it was very good – he had a very good self-editing mechanism.'

The second album, *What We Did On Our Holidays*, marks the emergence of Richard Thompson as a writer of awesome potential, and the beginning of what Robin Denselow later called 'Folkrock Brittanicus' (in the shape of 'Nottamun Town' and 'She Moves Through The Fair').

Meet On The Ledge

It also includes Ian Matthews' best-remembered song with the band – 'Book Song' – and demonstrates just how well Fairport were assimilating their internal and external influences. The album's cover is from a blackboard in the band's dressing room, decimated before a gig at Essex University (the title being a parody of a standard English school essay subject).

It is remarkably mature for a second album, the diversity of the outside material – Dylan and Joni Mitchell – balancing with the band's own compositions, and their interpretations of the traditional songs.

An original Sandy Denny song opens the album, the beautiful lament 'Fotheringay', written after Sandy visited the castle of Fotheringay in Northamptonshire, where Mary Queen of Scots was executed in February 1587. The song's beauty is enhanced by the weaving acoustic guitars of Sandy and Richard and Ashley's looping bass. It proved just how well Sandy suited Fairport, her soaring, sensitive voice coaxing the band to fresh heights. It was, of course, the song after which Sandy christened her own band when she split from Fairport.

'Mr Lacey' was Ashley Hutchings' only solo composition with the band, written some three years previously about his neighbour in Durnsford Road, the eccentric Prof. Bruce Lacey, the man who put on 'Evenings Of British Rubbish' in London theatres. Worldwide fame, however, eluded the professor, even after playing the Beatles' indoor gardener in *Help!*, and he returned to his life-sized stuffed camel in North London. Ian: 'Tyger said, "I'm bringing him down to play the solo." And it turned out that the solo was three robots walking about making that noise. Oh, and he wore a space suit to the session too!'

Ian already had the words and melody for 'Book Song', and Richard simply wrote the chords for it. Ian: 'It's a song about my wife, although she wasn't my wife at the

2 She Moves Through The Fair

time. I just compared life to being like a book.' The cello on the track was played by Clare Lowther, wife of jazz trumpeter Henry Lowther, who also established a Fairport connection when he played on *Gottle O'Geer* seven years later.

'The Lord Is In This Place, How Dreadful Is This Place' is a re-working of Blind Willie Johnson's 'Dark Was The Night, Cold Was The Ground' and was recorded in the evenings (to avoid traffic noise) at St Peter's Church, Westbourne Grove. Simon: 'We were interested in using the various possibilities open to us, one of which was Richard playing slide guitar on a moody song.'

The coins heard on the track were dropped by Kingsley Abbott, and the disappearing footsteps belong to Martin Lamble. (It was to this echoingly spatial song that Greil Marcus referred in his *Rolling Stone* obituary of Sandy Denny, which ended 'and I doubt if I am the only fan of Sandy Denny's who thought of it when I heard that she had died'.)

The following song on the album marked Richard Thompson's debut as a solo writer, and on the evidence of 'No Man's Land' alone, it should have been obvious to all but the deaf in heart that here was a writer of substance. (The New Seekers thought so when they recorded the song on their 1971 *Colours* album, a track on which – it is alleged – Richard Thompson plays guitar!) In the very first issue of *Zig Zag* – which featured Fairport on its cover – Pete Frame gave the album an ecstatic write-up, calling 'No Man's Land' 'an exuberant accordion dominated romp, which, despite the despondent lyric, conjures up visions of leather-trousered, dancing Germans spilling beer'. (Thompson was the accordion player, and it was in that capacity, under the Marxian pseudonym Wolf J. Flywheel, that he appeared on Ian Matthews' 1972 album *Tigers Will Survive*.)

As always with Fairport, their interpretations of other

21

writers' material was impeccable, and their lengthy workout on Dylan's 'I'll Keep It With Mine' is exemplary. Dylan allegedly wrote it for Nico while she was hanging around New York circa 1964, and recorded it himself for his fourth album with simple piano accompaniment (his version has never been officially released), but Fairport's rich rendering swells the song to something approaching greatness (just listen to Sandy's singing on the last verse, particularly the section: 'The conductor, he's still stuck on the line . . .'). An inspired version of a little known song by one of Fairport's perennial influences. And that's only the first side of the album!

Although Joni Mitchell's first album was now available, she was still quite an unknown quantity in the UK, and Fairport's cover of her 'Eastern Rain' benefits from a lavish arrangement with Lamble's drums to the fore, and a gorgeous, tight, Thompson solo. It is, however, the following track, 'Nottamun Town', which is of particular interest in hindsight. Ashley claims it was a song known to the band before Sandy joined, through Jean Ritchie and Shirley Collins (in fact Fairport's arrangement stays remarkably close to the Davy Graham/Shirley Collins arrangement on their seminal 1964 *Folk Roots, New Routes* album). But the Fairport version is enriched by the massed, doomy voices chanting the eerie 'Ten thousand was drownded that never was born' section. The electricity on the song was muted, but set the scene, even though it was an acoustic Thompson solo and Matthews' congas which gave the song its Eastern air.

The second Thompson composition on the album, 'Tale In Hard Time', displays the composer's predilection for doom, which has stayed with him throughout his composing career. Although set to a jaunty tune, lines like: 'Take the sun from my heart, let me learn to disguise' evince Thompson's fascination with the dark side of the human condition.

2 She Moves Thr...

But it was on Margaret Barry's arrangement of ... Moves Through The Fair' (erroneously credited as a 'traditional' song, as it is based on a poem by Padraic Colum) that Fairport's obvious experimentations began. It was a song Sandy had sung solo around the clubs before she joined Fairport, and was one of the songs suggested during one of the band's periodic get-togethers to discuss what new material to include. Simon: 'It was not put on as a sop to Sandy, but we wanted something that was representative of what she was doing in the clubs ... It's a bit of a nothing arrangement.'

Ashley: 'She Moves Through The Fair' was basically Sandy's working, and us just fitting in around her. If you actually took out the tracks with the drums and electric bass and electric guitars, you would have Sandy doing it exactly as she would do it in the clubs anyway.' Although the electricity and arrangement were muted, 'She Moves Through The Fair' gave a tantalising indication of the direction in which Fairport were moving.

The album's penultimate track was another ace up the Fairport sleeve, and another solo Richard Thompson composition – 'Meet On The Ledge'. It is a song inexorably associated with Fairport Convention, entwined with tragic memories of Martin Lamble. A song of depth, of parting and reunion, a song of premonition and eventual hope. It is a song only Richard Thompson could have written, and to which only Fairport Convention could do justice (although Noel Murphy and Prelude both covered it competently enough).

It was also their first Island single, released towards the end of November 1968, and was included on the first Island sampler *You Can All Join In*. Typically, Richard Thompson cannot recall the circumstances surrounding the song's creation, save that material was needed to complete the *Holidays* album. Brian Wyvill, though, is almost certain it was written for Thompson's

William Ellis School. Wyvill feels the
[...] with the Pothole Tree on Hampstead
[...] he young Thompson, with Wyvill and
[...] ain, would climb after school. Wyvill later
[...] complished mountaineer. (Indeed, he was
work[...] a volume entitled 'The History Of Mountaineering In Patagonia' when I met him!) During those schoolboy tree climbing episodes, he and Quartermain would usually get right to the top, but the trepidatious Thompson would only get to a branch halfway up – The Ledge.

A reunion was set between the three for 1 April 1972, to see what changes had been rung since the days of the old schoolyard, but Brian Wyvill was abroad on that date, and never did find out if it took place. He feels that the song is certainly associated with that event, which does tie in with its feel of resigned optimism. ('You'll have your chance again, and you can do the work for me.')

Fairport's performance is nothing short of superb – Ian and Sandy trading heartfelt verses, while the rest of the band swing in on the chorus. It was a song played at Martin Lamble's funeral, and not played on stage by Fairport until their 'Farewell' tour of 1979 (and enshrined on the otherwise lamentable *Farewell, Farewell* album). It was also disinterred for their second farewell performance at Cropredy in 1980, when Fairport Mark 15 were joined on stage by Richard and Linda Thompson.

Of the single, *Disc And Music Echo* said: 'It's a hit with me personally, but could get lost in the Christmas rush,' and *Melody Maker*'s inimitable Chris Welch called it: 'A stand-out performance by a most under-rated group ... This is one for the discerning.'

Ian: 'We were going round the circuit and seeing all the bands, and they were all saying, "Yes, that's a great single, that's going to do it." I think that was my first disappointment, when "Meet On The Ledge" didn't happen.'

2 She Moves Through The Fair

What We Did On Our Holidays finishes with Simon Nicol's pensive 'End Of A Holiday', a tune he wrote to a set of Ian's lyrics, 'Billy Gives In'. Although Simon's tune and Ian's words didn't gel, the tune was kept and tagged on as an effective end to the album. 'Maybe as a sop to me,' says Simon.

Also recorded for the *Holidays* album, but never released, was a version of Dylan's 'Dear Landlord'.

Holidays is an impressive progression from their Polydor debut, and a fascinating example of the half a dozen directions which that particular Fairport could have followed. As John Wood remembered in his sleeve notes to *History Of . . .*: 'The whole group was into using the studio as much as possible.' This is amply testified to on the album, with its use of multi-tracking: Clare Lowther's cello on 'Book Song', Richard's accordion on 'No Man's Land', Bruce Lacey's robots and Nicol's violin on 'Nottamun Town'. Simon: 'We're talking about textures. All of us were interested in multi-tracking, like on "Nottamun Town", this little patch of double-stopping on the fiddle, even if it came out of nowhere and was never seen again, we'd do it.' Nicol's fiddling is best described as 'enthusiastic' – he professes little more than a rudimentary knowledge of the instrument: 'At the end of "Jack O'Diamonds" on stage, I'd talk about how I'd had to unlearn all my technique, pull faces and play "avant garde" fiddle – as in "avant garde a clue how to play it!'

What We Did On Our Holidays was released in January 1969, and gained considerable attention for the group, most critics favourably remarking on their progression. That same month Al Stewart's *Love Chronicles* was also released, on which Ashley played bass, Richard and Simon played guitars (Richard under the Shadowy pseudonym Marvin Prestwick, with Simon thinly disguised as Simon Breckenridge) and Martin Lamble on drums, credited as Martin Francis.

Meet On The Ledge

The band were clearly delighted with the results of the album, but ructions were ahead. Ian Matthews was obviously pleased with 'Book Song', which he saw as 'definitely an indication of where I wanted to go ... and that was the direction that I thought the band were going to go, and that was what I was working on'. But the injection of Sandy's traditional material from the folk clubs coincided with Ashley's growing interest in exploring that particularly rich seam.

Coupled with those developments was the burgeoning of Sandy and Richard as writers, something which Ian was clearly aware of: 'Richard's a unique kind of person. He could tie all that stuff in, the traditional side of it and the contemporary side of it, and make it all sound like one thing, like it all belongs in the same place ... I could never do that.' The signs were that Fairport and Ian Matthews were growing apart. Although he did sing on 'Percy's Song' for their proposed third album, the disparity became apparent when the band booked a session to record a traditional song without telling him. Ian: 'I was just a singer in the band. I didn't have any input on the kind of songs we did, that was Richard and Ashley ... I think I did know the kind of stuff that I *didn't* really want to do. You know, I never enjoyed going into that traditional stuff, it was alien to me. There was no place for me to take part in something like that because I didn't have any kind of traditional roots like Sandy, and I didn't have any traditional sense like Richard and Ashley did, and I didn't have any interest in it ... It became increasingly clear that there was really no place for me in a band playing that type of music ... I think I probably intimidated them a little by making it clear, up until when they went into the studio without me to record a traditional song, that really pissed me off. I didn't like that at all, and the next thing I knew Joe Boyd told me they wanted me to leave the band.'

2 She Moves Through The Fair

In the lengthy John Tobler *Zig Zag* piece published seven years after he left the band, Matthews recalled: 'I did have regrets about leaving, but at the same time I'm glad I did, because the next two albums were amazing albums that I could never have taken part in.

'I could have taken part in some of *Unhalfbricking*, but *Liege & Leif* was just way beyond what I was into.' So Ian Matthews was cursorily, but not unexpectedly, asked to leave the band, although he continued to share the Brent flat with Richard and Martin.

Within months of leaving Fairport, Matthews found himself at number one in the British charts with his band Southern Comfort and their version of Joni Mitchell's 'Woodstock'. He did occasionally venture back and sing with Fairport for about a year after having officially left, as at a Little Hadham police benefit, where he contributed a – by all accounts – ragged version of 'Meet On The Ledge'. On the dissolution of Southern Comfort, Matthews formed the excellent, but short-lived, Plainsong. He recorded a number of solo albums in the States, produced by such luminaries as ex-Monkee Mike Nesmith and Nashville sessionman Norbert Putnam, but real popular success has seemingly eluded him.

1980 saw the release of an excellent new album, *Spot Of Interference*, and a tastefully compiled double album, *Discreet Repeat*, which chronicled the best of Matthews' solo work. Of interest was his version of Richard Farina's 'Reno, Nevada', which of course he used to sing with Fairport. The album displays Matthews' voice at its best, particularly on his covers of songs by Tom Waits and Tim Hardin. Back in 1969, Fairport Convention had acquired quite a reputation on the underground circuit and were gigging extensively, going out for about £600 a night. They were expanding their venues now, moving on from the underground haunts and carving a niche on the university circuit, which meant interminable drags up and down the motorways in draughty transit vans. They had gigged abroad, in Montreux and at the International Pop Festival in Rome, where Simon – because of his tender years – had to get a licence issued under the 'Young Persons Employment Abroad' act. The Bow Street magistrate noted that: 'The young person whilst abroad during the continuance of this licence, shall be in the personal charge of Mr Ashley Hutchings'!

It was during those fatiguing motorway journeys that the title for Fairport's – as yet unrecorded – third album came about. *Unhalfbricking* comes from a word game – 'Ghosts' – where the object of the game is to avoid completing a word. 'Unhalfbricking' was one of Sandy's efforts.

The years 1968/69 saw Fairport still heavily under their initial American influences, with the English traditional material merely a part of their repertoire. They played at the Royal Festival Hall in September 1968, along with Jackson C. Frank, Joni Mitchell and Al Stewart, as part of 'An Evening Of Contemporary Songs'. This was one of the strengths of Fairport around this time – their diversity. Their home-grown reputation meant that no one still thought of them as an American band, and they were drawing together the strands of traditional English folk music, material from American singer/songwriters, and the songs the band themselves were writing, although as writers, the band generally lacked confidence in their own material.

It was before a university gig that the epochal 'A Sailor's Life' came into being. Ashley: 'We were in a dressing room at Southampton University waiting to go on stage, and Sandy was playing around in the dressing room, and picked up the guitar and played and sang "Sailor's Life". We loved it, and said "Let's do that." We picked up our instruments and joined in – we had a little tuner amplifier in the dressing room, and we busked

2 She Moves Through The Fair

along. Then the time came to go on stage. We made an instant decision, I mean, we were all buzzing with that because we enjoyed doing it so much ... "Let's get out there and at it!" '

Joe: 'I first heard "Sailor's Life" at the Colston Hall in Bristol ... And it was clear to me that this was a new departure for them ... I remember being quite impressed and amazed by it.'

3 How Dreadful is this Place

It was while the band were in the process of recording their third album that there occurred the tragedy which – literally – scarred the band for years to come, and had an incalculable effect on their music. Fairport had finished a gig at Mother's in Birmingham with Eclection, and were heading towards London on the M1 motorway in the early hours of 12 May 1969. Sandy had driven back with Eclection's Trevor Lucas, and the rest of the band – Ashley, Richard, Simon and Martin – were being driven back in the group's 35 cwt transit by roadie Harvey Bramham. Also in the van was a friend of the band's, Jeannie (The Tailor) Franklyn, a cousin of Phil Ochs and a clothes designer who numbered the Doors among her clients.

Although still legally under age, Simon frequently used to share the late-night driving with Bramham, but he had felt a migraine coming on during the gig, and had gone straight to sleep on the floor of the van, right in front of the group's equipment. Bramham had been feeling ill all day, and on the way back to London had stopped off at the Watford Gap service area for some milk to try to calm his stomach.

The actual details of the crash are still vague, although what apparently happened was that Bramham fell asleep while driving and the van veered off the motorway. Richard, who was in the front seat next to Bramham,

3 How Dreadful is this Place

grabbed the wheel, but over-corrected, and the van cartwheeled. Simon: 'I can remember waking up while the van was actually somersaulting . . . When I woke up, I was the only one in the vehicle; everyone else had gone through windows and doors.' Nicol survived because the equipment shot out through the doors at the back of the van, rather than forward, which would have crushed him to death.

Harvey Bramham had gone straight through the windscreen and ended up about 90 feet away from the overturned vehicle. Richard and Ashley were wandering around dazed, and Martin was lying very still in the distance. Simon, who escaped virtually unscathed, managed to flag down a passing truck, the driver of which dashed over to the nearby Scratchwood service area to get help.

Eventually, after what seemed like hours and hours, the ambulances came and took the band to the Royal National Orthopaedic Hospital in Stanmore. Simon: 'I remember hours and hours of waiting in Casualty, where they were struggling with Martin. Jeannie was already dead when they put her in the ambulance . . . Richard just sat looking at the wall. Hutch couldn't see 'cos he had so much blood on his face . . . They only had to pick one tiny piece of glass out of my arm . . . I rang Anthea (Joseph) at Witchseason the next morning, glad of something to do.'

Anthea Joseph came up immediately with Martin's father, and threw the Drugs Squad out of the ward where the band were being kept.

Apparently, in the wreckage of the van the police had found – amidst the equipment which was strewn hundreds of yards up the motorway – a tiny box which contained some hash. Harvey Bramham was prosecuted for 'Causing death by dangerous driving', and served a term in prison.

Ashley: 'I had a broken nose, a broken cheek bone. I couldn't see immediately after the crash; both my eyes were closed up . . . When Ian came up to visit us, the first time he saw my face, he fainted on the next bed.' Joe Boyd was in the States at the time of the crash, where he had been playing the tapes of *Unhalfbricking* to the board of the Newport Folk Festival, and was in the process of arranging for Fairport to make their American debut at the Newport Festival of 1969. 'I felt at the time the group, as it was constituted for *Unhalfbricking*, was going to do very well in America. In fact, I was on my way to the West Coast to see Bill Graham about putting them on at the Fillmore when I got the call from London about the crash, and I turned around and flew back to London.'

The effect on the band was obviously shattering, but if anything it affected the people around them even worse, as the immediacy of the tragedy had passed for Fairport. Simon: 'The band had *been* through the worst thing that could have happened to them.' Many benefits were held for Fairport, notably one at London's Roundhouse where Pink Floyd, John Martyn and Eclection played, and one by King Crimson in Cornwall. The Beatles sent a telegram of commiseration.

Simon went with his girlfriend and Joe Boyd to Los Angeles for a fortnight to recuperate. A&M (Fairport's American record label) arranged for Sandy and Richard also to fly over to recover, and Richard stayed at Phil Ochs's house in LA. Jeannie Franklyn was commemorated on record later that year, when Jack Bruce dedicated his first solo album, *Songs For a Tailor*, to her memory.

Martin Lamble was cremated at Golders Green crematorium, and his ashes were scattered from a mountain in North Wales where the Lamble family had enjoyed many holidays. Kingsley Abbott helped Mr Lamble organise the funeral, Fairport's 'Meet On The Ledge' was played, and the verses chosen were the third chapter of Ecclesiastes: 'To every thing there is a season, and a time to every purpose under the heaven . . .' On Fairport Convention's

3 How Dreadful is this Place

first press release, under 'Previous Occupations', Martin Lamble had simply written: 'Child'.

The tragedy of the crash had a traumatic effect on Fairport Convention, as one would expect of any such closely knit group, the majority of whom were still barely into their twenties. Joe Boyd had the finished tapes of *Unhalfbricking*, which was released while Fairport were still recuperating, their future uncertain. The album eventually made it into the Top 20, but no one then knew if Fairport Convention were to continue as a band. Simon: 'We deliberately decided in Casualty that we weren't going to decide what to do when we knew Martin was dead.' Ashley: 'The crash was fundamentally important because it made up our minds for us, the path to be taken ... So it came to the point of actually sitting down and deciding what we were going to do. And this I remember clearly, we had a meeting at Trevor's flat with the survivors, Sandy, Richard, Simon and myself. We made a decision that we were going to re-form.'

Dave Swarbrick was asked in as a full-time member, having guested on *Unhalfbricking*, and drummers were auditioned in a room over a pub in Chiswick High Street, from whence emerged Fairport's new drummer – David James Mattacks.

Mattacks' pre-Fairport career had been the most diverse and unlikely of any of the band's members. Born in Edgware, London in March 1948, he took up the drums when he was 14, and struggled with early bands like the Pioneers, and Andy And The Marksmen. He then became a drummer for a professional dance band in Belfast for nine months, and Glasgow for two years. Simon: 'We were so lucky finding DM ... He was diligent, clean, used to taking three white shirts to a gig ... The application he could bring to his playing was amazing. With us, you only played well when you were feeling well.'

In a July 1980 interview with *Acoustic Music*, Mattacks

remembered the circumstances of his joining Fairport: 'There was, I think, Richard, Simon, Ashley and a drum kit. There was me and about half a dozen other guys. At the end of that, Simon said, "Do you want to come down to Winchester?" I did ... After 24 hours, Ashley said, "Do you want to join the group?" I said, "Yes, but I must tell you I haven't a fucking clue of what you're on about. I don't know anything about the music, I don't understand it ... I can't tell one tune from another, they all sound the same ... but if you want me to join the group, fine, because I really like it. I'm enjoying myself musically." '

As a complete contrast to Mattacks' rather shadowy pre-Fairport career, David Cyril Eric Swarbrick bounced into the band trailing his laurels behind him. Swarb was born in London in April 1941, but spent his early years in Birmingham. He obtained his City and Guilds at Birmingham College of Art, with the intention of becoming a printer. But it was the roving life for him, as a milkman and labourer. Music had been an abiding interest, and his first professional gig was with Beryl Marriot's Ceilidh Band. From there he progressed to a four-year stint with the Ian Campbell Folk Group, establishing a daemonic reputation as a violinist.

But it was his fruitful collaboration with Martin Carthy which gained him an unequalled reputation on the folk circuits, and the years spent working with the influential Carthy helped him acquire an extensive knowledge of traditional material. After half a dozen or so albums and innumerable gigs with Carthy, Swarb was growing frustrated with the limiting confines of the trad. folk scene, and was delighted when Joe Boyd rang and asked him down – initially for an over-dub on 'Cajun Woman' – to play with Fairport on *Unhalfbricking*. (Ken Hunt of *Swing 51* magazine remembers Family bassist/violinist Rick Grech helping Fairport out on some BBC sessions, shortly before Swarbrick's arrival.)

3 How Dreadful is this Place

Joe: 'It was either me or Sandy, I don't remember, who suggested him ... They were all very impressed with Swarbrick, very much of the attitude "Could we really get The Great Swarbrick to play?" ... I said I didn't think there was any problem at all ... I figured he would be delighted at the chance to play on a rock album and get the session fee.' Swarb was already suffering from the hearing problem which was to dog him over the years on the day he attended the first *Unhalfbricking* session. Ironically, he initially found that playing in front of an electric band actually *helped* his hearing, but years of playing with Fairport eventually made it impossible for him to play in an electric band, which led, of course, to Fairport knocking it on the head in 1979.

Something pretty dramatic was needed to unify Fairport after the crash, and the decision to pursue the possibilities suggested by 'A Sailor's Life' was the most exciting option, and was confirmed when Swarb was asked in full time. Swarbrick was personally pleased at being able to leave the traditional scene behind him, as he explained to Robin Denselow in *The Electric Muse*: 'I didn't like seven-eighths of the people involved in it, and it was exceedingly opportune to leave. I was suddenly presented with the possibilities of exploring the dramatic content of the songs to the full.' (Another more immediate reason may well have been financial: Swarb told me once that on joining Fairport, Joe Boyd told him he need only play 12 gigs with the band before he could afford to retire! Swarb went on to become Fairport's longest-serving member.)

In a *Melody Maker* interview with Tony Wilson shortly before he joined Fairport in 1969, Swarb enthused about the possibilities of working with them: 'A lot of the music we'll be doing will be very loosely folk. It will be based on traditional music, not just an electric copy. It's just the Fairport sound really ... We might take a traditional song and put it in the middle and say, "What can we do with it?" What we'd probably do is rewrite it.' Swarb also promised Wilson that the next Fairport album would be 'quite heavy on traditional material'.

Martin Carthy can remember an exuberant Swarbrick returning from an early *Unhalfbricking* session enthusing about the excitement of playing an electric duet with Richard Thompson. Simon: 'We did discuss the possibility of Martin Carthy joining at that time, but we thought it would be too top heavy, too many people involved . . . I didn't like the idea of *three* guitarists, particularly two like Richard and Martin!'

Unhalfbricking was released in July 1969, and if *Liege & Lief* was to be Fairport's *Sergeant Pepper*, then *Unhalfbricking* could well be compared with *Rubber Soul*. It is an album which demonstrates their uniqueness, fusing traditional English folk song, covering Bob Dylan songs and showcasing the brilliance of their two main writers – Sandy Denny and Richard Thompson. It could be said to be Fairport's last link with their own colourful and varied past, a restless, loving farewell to what had gone before.

The album opens with a spellbinding Richard Thompson song, 'Genesis Hall', named after a squat near the Arts Lab in Drury Lane, from which the police were in the process of evicting the squatters who had renovated the derelict building. Thompson's father was still serving in the police force at the time, which goes some way towards explaining the ambiguity of the song's opening lines: 'My father he rides with your sheriffs/And I know he would never mean harm . . .' It conjures up images of Scottish border raids in the 17th century, and it's hard to believe the composer was only 20 years old. The effect of his and Sandy's voices swelling on the chorus – 'Oh, oh, helpless and slow/And you don't have anywhere to go' – is beautiful, infusing the song with a Gothic solemnity. (It is also one of the few songs Thompson wrote for Fairport that he and Linda included for many years in their stage set.)

3 **How Dreadful is this Place**

'Si Tu Dois Partir' is the first of three Dylan songs on the album, almost their final homage to one of the band's seminal influences. It was Fairport's only hit single, resulting in their unforgettable appearance on *Top Of The Pops*: Richard on accordion, Ashley playing an enormous double bass with a French loaf, trying to out-beret Mattacks on washboard and roadie Steve Sparks on percussion. The more discerning reader may recall that Manfred Mann had a hit with the same song, 'If You Gotta Go, Go Now', in 1965, differing only slightly from Fairport's version in that it was sung in English! The French translation was one of those spontaneous decisions they delighted in. Ashley: 'It was one of those things which was characteristic ... Sitting in a dressing room thinking, what are we going to do? Why don't we do it in French? Why don't we do it *now*! ... We were very impetuous, and we were also very sparky, and I think that – certainly in recent years I have not known this – there was a certain feeling with that band, of experimentation and energy.'

Richard remembers Fairport were doing a gig at Middle Earth and thought it would be fun to do Dylan's song in French cajun manner, so the DJ broadcast over the PA asking if there was a Frenchman in the house! 'About three people turned up, so it was really written by committee, and consequently ended up not very cajun, French or Dylan!' (Dylan allegedly repaid the compliment by recording a version of Thompson's 'Farewell, Farewell' for *Self Portrait* in 1970, but the song was dropped in favour of 'The Boxer'.)

'Autopsy' was an early, jazz-influenced Sandy song, and side one was wrapped up with the 11-minute 'A Sailor's Life', a firm indication that Fairport were voyaging into hitherto unexplored areas. The song is an 18th-century broadside ballad which Sandy had learnt from A. L. (Bert) Lloyd. Ashley had apparently been burrowing around in the library of Cecil Sharp House, and had come up with subsequent verses. The band were delighted with the success of the song on stage, and wanted their version, complete with sweeping electric jam, included on the album.

They ran through the song once in the studio, Swarbrick joining in, playing his acoustic fiddle straight into the microphone. They then recorded it straight through onto tape which, apart from one tiny edit at the end, is the version that finished up on *Unhalfbricking*. It was the fourth song they recorded that Sunday afternoon, and Sandy was isolated in a glass booth, with only a streaming cold for company, to record the vocal. 'It didn't,' recalled Simon 11 years later, 'look auspicious.' But Fairport's radical reworking of the song ('authenticated' by Swarb's presence) surged electricity into the moribund English folk movement.

What is remarkable about the song is how, after Sandy's languid vocals have told the tale of her 'sweet William', the band swing in and finish the song with a brooding, electric jam. Hutchings' sturdy bass swells in unison with Lamble's rolling drums, as Richard and Swarb cross swords and bring the song to its crashing climax.

Ashley: 'They set the tape rolling and we did it, and the energy and adrenalin were incredible. When we finished, we knew what we had done ... we went into the box to hear it. Joe and John were almost speechless ... we *knew* we had done something different. We knew that here was a path open to us which hadn't previously been clear.'

Simon: 'The purity of the original song is not watered down by the arrangement ... We thought about extending ourselves musically, beginning to realise what an asset Sandy was, with her access to traditional material and, of course, her own writing ... I felt very honoured that Swarb came in – it lent folk authenticity.'

3 How Dreadful is this Place

Everyone – the band, Joe Boyd and John Wood – was delighted with the result. It marked a quantum leap from their first tentative experiment on 'She Moves Through The Fair' a year before. Suddenly the possibilities of 'folk rock' seemed limitless. Fairport were no longer dipping cautious toes into the reservoir of traditional material, but had plunged in up to their necks.

In a piece in *Disc*, John Peel called the song 'one of the best things I've ever heard', and waxed lyrical for half a page about the album. His comments on 'A Sailor's Life' are, I feel, worth repeating, because they capture so perfectly the enthusiasm which Fairport's arrangement aroused, and also for the sensitivity of Peel's writing: 'The opening of "A Sailor's Life" is soft with breezes and sunshine and sea guitar. Just gentle and stroked and so good... The wind builds and Dave Swarbrick is suddenly there on violin while Martin rolls the stones on the sea-bed. Simon and Richard come and go as the sun does. Now we're being driven along by a fine wind and the bow cuts through the rolling sea on the edge of Richard's guitar and Dave's violin... Now Tyger is there on my right and the whole wondrous crew is sailing into calmer waters on a cymbal breeze. About eleven minutes among some islands and flying fish. Recorded, too, in one take without overdubbing, because you can't re-take voyages like that.'

The voyage continued on side two of the album with a Thompson diversion into Louisiana territory. (In Rodney Crowell's words, 'It's alligator bait and the bars don't close.') Thompson has always had an abiding fascination with cajun – the hillbilly/folk-based, French-influenced music native to the New Orleans area – and his 'Cajun Woman' employs the band to great effect on accordion, fiddle, percussion and slide guitar, sounding as authentic as a bunch of Londoners can expect to sound on a type of music virtually confined to the Everglades.

Meet On The Ledge

Judy Collins ensured Sandy comfortable royalties for years to come when she recorded 'Who Knows Where The Time Goes' for the soundtrack of the Martin Sheen film *The Subject Was Roses*, and also as the title track of her eighth album. It is a classic Sandy song, plaintive without coming across as self-pitying. A song of the seasons, of stark, autumnal imagery, warmed by the fireside comfort of Sandy's poignant performance. A writer coming to terms with the fragility of emotion, one who holds no fear of time, who does not mourn its passing due to the comfort derived from the inevitability of its return. A song for dreamers and for those in love, and for those who wished they were in love with that sort of intensity. Sandy's peerless, perfectly enunciated vocals do the song the sort of justice it merits.

'Percy's Song' is Dylan circa 1964, but his own simple guitar-accompanied version palls beside Richard's majestic arrangement, as the massed Fairport voices (including Ian Matthews) sing the tale of friendship blighted by an iniquitous 'justice'. The song builds with dignity as the narrative unfolds, as the friend confronts the impassive Kafkaesque judge in his chambers, simply lamenting the fact that 'he ain't no criminal', a drama played out against the unremitting, cruel rain and the wind.

Simon: 'It needs a voice like Sandy's to get the shades of emotion across, from moodiness to compassion to outright fury. There's not many singers can do that.' So true, particularly of her handling of the last verse, as the singer 'plays his guitar through the night and the day', achieving some sort of uneasy tranquillity through his music. 'Percy's Song' was meant to be the single from the album, but was felt – at nearly seven minutes – to be too long.

'Million Dollar Bash', from the infamous 1967 *Basement Tapes* wraps the album up in grand party mood. Again, it was recorded straight through in one take, and

3 How Dreadful is this Place

is notable for Ashley's curious approximation of an American accent on the second verse.

John Mendelsohn in *Rolling Stone* called the album 'Fairport Convention at its best', and extolled the virtues of Thompson as a writer, although he was far from happy about the lengthy 'Sailor's Life'.

Fusion magazine called it 'perfect', and compared it in terms of impact to *Astral Weeks* and *Music From Big Pink*.

A&M felt that the English cover, Sandy's parents in the foreground, while the group were seen taking tea in their garden, was unacceptable to American audiences. So they replaced it with an extraordinary picture of a procession of elephants, seemingly intent on sodomy, with a ballet dancer pirouetting atop the herd, which to my mind says something *very* interesting about the American psyche!

While Fairport were recuperating after the crash, Joe Boyd rented the band an enormous Queen Anne mansion in Farley Chamberlayne, about 11 miles outside Winchester. It was there they lived, fully absorbed Swarb into the band, and rehearsed the material which would eventually constitute the *Liege & Lief* album. They did not, though, concentrate solely on electrifying traditional material. Ashley remembers they 'kept the thread with Dylan', working out a version of 'Open The Door, Homer', which never saw the light of day, and 'Down In The Flood', which was never recorded at the time, but did surface on Sandy's first solo album some three years later (and in 1974, on the *Fairport Live Convention* album). Roger McGuinn's 'Ballad Of Easy Rider' *was* recorded, and turned up on Richard's 1976 *Guitar, Vocal* compilation – its inclusion on *Liege & Lief* would have been incongruous, to say the least! Richard Farina's 'Quiet Joys Of Brotherhood' was also recorded, but again did not appear on the finished album. A different version did surface, however, on Sandy's second solo album in 1972.

But the majority of the band's six-month incubation there was spent in arranging traditional songs for a five-piece electric rock band. Simon remembered the first Sweeney's Men album as being a great influence on the group at that time – 'Folk music with the frills taken off.' The input of material came mainly from Sandy and Swarb, but with Ashley, Richard and Simon taking a creative role in adapting and arranging.

Simon: 'I can remember three sets of Child books in the house at any one time ... I'm sure the beetle-browed Hutchings had it all planned ... DM was getting a tremendous charge out of it, inventing a whole new form of drumming without knowing it ... Martin's strength was as an imaginative drummer. DM came with a strongly developed sense of rhythm, through keeping a big band of drunken saxophone players in order. A great timekeeper.'

Fairport *needed* a challenge that summer, to unify the band in the aftermath of the crash, something to help them forge ahead rather than tread water. While satisfied with their previous albums, the band were obviously stimulated by Swarbrick's inclusion, and felt that the direction indicated by 'A Sailor's Life' could be improved and expanded over a complete album. They wanted to wipe the dust off the shelf marked 'Folk', and bring it all back home.

4 Trad. Arr. Fairport

Fairport Convention did not 'invent' folk rock or electric folk. They were simply intuitive enough to seize disparate elements – traditional 'folk' music and rock 'n' roll – and breathe new life into them by fusing the two together.

Others had tried. Pentangle, formed in 1967, utilised the talents of those two unique guitarists, John Renbourn and Bert Jansch, the jazz background of drummer Terry Cox, double bassist Danny Thompson, and the purity of singer Jacquie McShee. Jansch and Renbourn were the best known, bringing with them a reputation forged in the folk clubs as brilliant guitarists. Jansch – cited by Zeppelin's Jimmy Page as a formative influence – was a distinctive writer too, and his 'Needle Of Death' became quite a folk club standard. Pentangle were certainly eclectic in their music. In concert they were quite apt to fuse folk, gospel and Thelonious Monk together, but they were emphatic in their eschewing of electric instruments, and remained acoustic until very late in their career.

They were managed by Jo Lustig, who later handled Fairport for a period, and who quickly brought Pentangle to an eminence their contemporaries could never match (their first 'proper' gig was at the Royal Festival Hall). They eventually split in 1972, with Jansch going on to work fruitfully with Mike Nesmith and with Renbourn in the excellent, but sadly sporadic John Renbourn Group, which amalgamated traditional music with Indian elements.

Virtually up until Fairport's vigorous reworkings of traditional material on *Liege & Lief*, folk music meant relatively little to contemporary audiences. Folk clubs conjured up pictures of stalwart (probably middle-aged) men, with a pint clasped in one beefy hand, the other clenched round an ear, grinding their way through interminable 40-verse ballads in a smoky room over a pub. Possessed of a certain charm, certainly, but with about as much relevance to the 20th century as the Peace of Utrecht!

It could be argued that without Fairport, folk music would still be a cult, condemned to garret rooms, for devotees only, semantically split between 'revivalists' and 'traditionalists', factions as entrenched and divided as Michael Foot's Labour Party. Fairport grabbed the bull by the horns and unceremoniously dragged the unwilling beast into the 20th century. They blasted their results through amplifiers more used to the urban poetry of Chuck Berry's 'Too Much Monkey Business' than the prosaic narrative of 'Tam Lin'. They exposed the tip of the iceberg to a generation for whom folk music meant little more than purgatorial primary school lessons, where the characters in the songs seemed to do little apart from 'rove out one May morning so early'!

Folk music is music for the people by the people, embodying a tradition in England stretching way back to when the Picts went on the woad. Ideally, it represents music unsullied by commercialism, an excuse for members of the community to relax, and hear contemporary news or narratives unfolded in song.

The music they heard was often indigenous to their village or area, and the songs spoke of their lives and aspirations, frequently providing an excuse to indulge in fantasies which few of them would ever realise. The songs were of the times – of war, of myth, of legend, of love, of life and (in inordinate detail) of death. But it was music that *lived*, music which was carried down through the generations, adapted and changed – not sterile texts, safely unmalleable in the domain of the scholar.

The Broadsheet ballads achieved great popularity during the latter half of the 18th century, but were at their apogee during Victorian times. They were songs composed about specific, contemporary incidents (frequently a murder or battle), and sold by travellers to small communities with no access to newspapers.

Folk music evokes an England destroyed by the Industrial Revolution: songs dating from medieval times, with clearly defined social roles, simple texts with rich melodies. The songs conjure up visions of merry peasants gambolling around the Maypole; sturdy yeomen off to fight and die in the service of the monarch; elaborate, colourful rituals to celebrate the coming of Spring; small, agrarian communities, reliant on the land for their living, never moving far from their homes, horizons limited to village, town and county.

The songs reflected the inflexibility of the social structure – the vassals paying their homage (lief) to the Lord of the Manor (the liege) – and from Magna Carta to the Industrial Revolution, they offer us a picture of an unchanging England. The ballads, though, were longer pieces, strong on narrative, often containing deceptively complex imagery and vivid use of language.

The 19th century saw the factories growing as the cities expanded. There, the wages were marginally better for agricultural labourers, and the railways spread like a spider's web, helping bring the workers closer to the factories, endangering and – in collusion with the internal combustion engine – eventually destroying the isolated, insulated villages. G. M. Trevelyan's *History Of England* notes: 'Up to the Industrial Revolution, economic and social change, though continuous, has the pace of a slowly moving stream; but in the days of Watt and Stephenson it has acquired the momentum of water over a mill-dam...' The population of England at this time was some 9,000,000, with approximately 3,000,000 of those engaged in agriculture, but 78% still *lived* in the country, and could therefore be seen as inheritors of the folk traditions.

The rural communities survived until the First World War took its fatal toll, leaving hardly one hamlet untouched by death. After the Great War, freedom of movement, radio, cinema and television effectively destroyed the culture of small communities.

Perhaps the vision of Eden before the Fall which the folk songs help conjure up today is mildly fanciful. But folk-myths perpetrated by the songs *do* survive – Robin Hood, Thomas the Rhymer, the False Knight on the Road, the Wandering Jew – and the songs, dances and traditions have passed into the rich field of 'Folk Culture'.

A great deal of the blame for the state of the folk music which survives today must be laid at the feet of the collectors and collators who laboured so hard in the latter half of the last century. Frequently it is their bowdlerised versions of the songs which survive – although intent on preserving the English heritage at all costs, they ensured that the songs were fit for the ears of prim Victorian ladies.

However grateful we may be to those eminent, scholarly gentlemen – the two most notable being Cecil Sharp and Francis Child, both of whom are pictured on the sleeve of *Liege & Lief* – it must be remembered that the versions of the songs they collected were not necessarily the songs as they were sung. Although frequently acquiring the songs first hand, their view was that they must be made 'suitable', which involved amending, deleting and, at times, completely rewriting the traditional songs.

It was only in 1954 that the International Folk Music Council was able to produce a definition of the music they had chosen to study: 'Folk music is the product of a musical tradition that has been evolved through the process of oral transmission.' It was that word 'oral' which produced the schisms which later marred the 'Folk Revival' of the 1960s. An interesting comment on that particular dilemma came from Tim Hart of Steeleye Span – a group who themselves did much to incur the wrath of the traditionalists – again from *The Electric Muse*: 'My personal philosophy is that most English traditional song is unaccompanied song, and the only argument is – should you or should you not accompany it at all? After that I'm not interested in any argument as to what degree you can go to. To me, it's equally outrageous to accompany a traditional song on a Spanish guitar or an American instrument as it is to accompany it with an electric guitar!'

'The Folk Revival' was a confused, frustrating, enchanted and exciting period. Suddenly, folk clubs were places to *be*, whether the Troubador, Cousins, or a room above 'The Cock' in St Albans. It really caught fire for the pre-Beatles crowd when visiting Americans came over and drew extensively on our traditional heritage (as with Dylan acquiring a tune for his own 'Bob Dylan's Dream' from Martin Carthy's arrangement of 'Lord Franklin').

The roots of the popular folk revival can be traced back to the skiffle boom of the mid-fifties. Skiffle was Britain's answer to American rock 'n' roll – home grown, but deriving in the main from the influential American troubadour Woody Guthrie. It was the *accessibility* of skiffle which gave it such an appeal, and Ashley Hutchings and Al Stewart were only two of many eminent British musicians who made obeisance towards Lonnie Donegan.

Britain lacked a comparable figure to Guthrie, although Ewan MacColl made a substantial contribution towards making a broader audience aware of folk's inherent possibilities. It took the sixties revival to bring folk down from the garrets and up from the basements. Fiery young stylists like Bert Jansch, Davy Graham and Al Stewart drew heavily on the folk tradition, while developing their own writing and expanding their musical parameters. A number of those early 'folkies' saw folk as simply one string to their bow, also learning from blues and rock in their search for a comprehensive, and frequently idiosyncratic, musical style.

But it divided the folk world. The traditionalists (those who abided by the Folk Music Council's dictum that folk music could only be learnt *orally*) were on the whole dismissive of the revivalists (those fired by the possibilities of folk music, unconcerned whether the songs came from other singers, or – sin of sins – from *records*).

Many and fascinating were the developments in the folk scene on both sides of the Atlantic during the early sixties. In America, disillusioned by the anodyne pop of Ricky Nelson, Bobby Vee and Brian Hyland, young contemporary singers turned to their own folk tradition of blues, bluegrass, country and Woody Guthrie. That disinterring of earlier musical forms resulted in the folk boom which produced the Greenwich Village renaissance, where Kerouac and Lenny Bruce performed alongside the innumerable singer/songwriters. Dylan, Richard Farina and Phil Ochs emerged from the creative lava thrown up by that particular eruption. An example of what could be achieved in popular terms was Alan Price's reworking of 'The House Of The Rising Sun', which reached number one here in 1964. It was that recording which opened up the eyes of Bob Dylan as to what could be achieved by fusing folk and rock, which is just what he did – much to the vexation of the folk establishment – at Newport the following year.

In England, Martin Carthy was the leading light on the revivalist side, combining a strong voice with a distinctive guitar style. Carthy endlessly sifted through manuscripts at Cecil Sharp House to obtain the definitive version of a traditional song. But perhaps the most fascinating album of that period was the 1964 *Folk Roots, New Routes*, which combined the eclectic guitarist Davy Graham with the traditional Sussex singer Shirley Collins. It is a real blotting pad of an album, soaking up everything from Thelonious Monk to Appalachian mountain music and back, via Cecil Sharp. If not demolishing the barriers, that album certainly broadened them considerably.

The 'Young Folk Rebels' felt that no song was sacrosanct, *particularly* if it was passed down orally through the generations. Changes – they reasoned – *must* occur during its transmission.

However venerable a song may be, it is as open to interpretation as a poem to the creative artist, who finds himself aware of the limitations imposed by the song's structure or lyric. The process of modifying could be seen as part of the creative process, tautening the narrative, enhancing the characterisation or finding a more suitable melody for the lyric. Often the traditional songs found themselves as little more than a foundation for a radical reworking. Obviously, however, opinions would always differ about the success of the interpretation.

Folk music can never die, but it can wither through lack of interest. It can become the property of a clique whose sole concern lies in preserving the song in aspic, so that it will pass unaltered down the years. The *Encyclopedia Brittanica*'s definition of folklore ran thus: 'Legend may be said to be distorted history. It contains a nucleus of historical fact, the memories of which have been elaborated or distorted by accretions derived from myth . . .' A number of revivalists felt that this 'distortion' could well be beneficial to a traditional song, without affecting either its merit or value. Their efforts differed from their Victorian predecessors, whose main concern seemed to be with the songs' propriety. The revivalists' amendments concentrated on making the song as alive as possible to modern ears.

There is certainly an argument in favour of the 'traditional' approach – to keep the music alive in as near its original form as possible. The restriction of that approach is that it has a tendency to isolate the music from the people for whom it is ostensibly being preserved, keeping the music within the realm of the scholar and purist.

To sustain interest in the music, it has to remain relevant to contemporary ears. The 'Preservation At All Costs' school could – and did – have an alienating effect upon the audience it was striving to reach.

One must in the end admire and thank the efforts of the collectors and staunch traditionalists, for without them the folk music of these islands would almost certainly have withered and died. But music, folk music in particular, must adapt to the times, and in the last half of the 20th century, it would be unrealistic and incongruous to ignore the technology now made available to a growing number of artists and performers.

Without wishing to get bogged down in the semantic swamp of what folk music actually *is*, I feel that in this day and age songs (as with all valid art) must mirror and reflect the society which produces them. Which is why the songs of a polemicist like Tom Robinson, working very much in the rock arena towards the end of the austere 1970s, could well still be considered 'folk' songs.

In the same way that rock 'n' roll can encompass the symphonic aspirations of Mike Oldfield *and* the amphetamine ardour of the Clash, folk music can embrace the untutored, unaccompanied singing of Harry Cox and the sophisticated beggarry of Roy Harper.

Fairport Convention's electric reworkings of the traditional songs stayed true to the spirit of the originals. If you compare an 'original' version of say, 'Banks Of The Sweet

Top: A very early Fairport gig, London, 1967. Left to right: Simon Nicol, Martin Lamble, Ashley Hutchings, Richard Thompson

Right: Later that same evening, Richard grows rock-star sunglasses

Below: The Fairport house and plaque

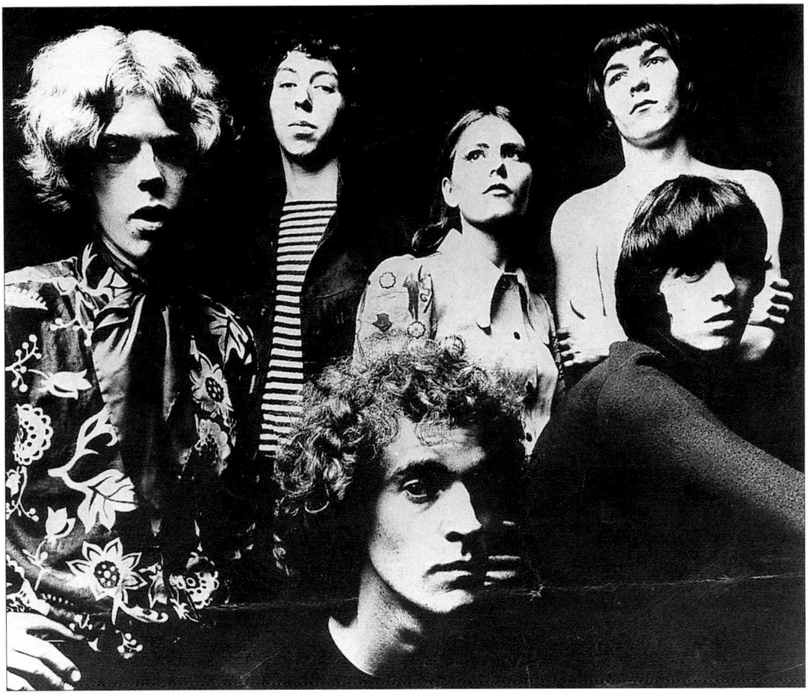

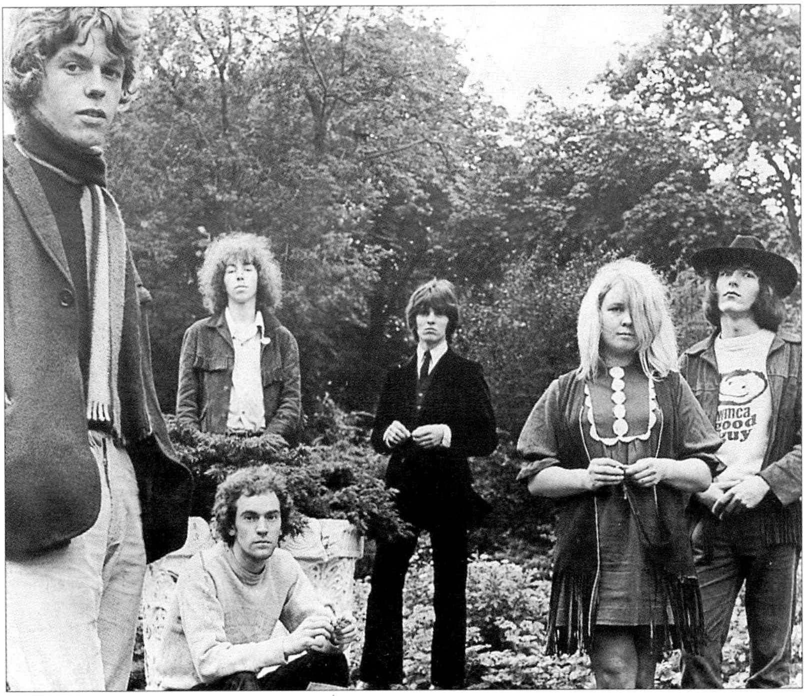

Opposite top: Fairport at the time of their first album, left to right: Martin Lamble, Richard Thompson, Ashley Hutchings, Judy Dyble, Simon Nicol, Ian Matthews

Opposite below: By the summer of 1968 Sandy Denny had replaced Judy Dyble

Above: Moody, Bergmanesque, and Ian Matthews gets the hat

Right: Fairport get it together in the country with assorted urchins, park-keepers and Witchseason's Anthea Joseph between Martin and Simon

Fairport drummer dies in M1 crash

FAIRPORT CONVENTION drummer Martin Lamble, and an American girl known as Jeanie The Tailor were killed when the group's van overturned and crashed on the M1 at Mill Hill on Monday morning.

The group were on the way back to London after a gig at Mother's Club in Birmingham.

Martin (19) and Jeanie, whose real name was Franklin, girl friend of Fairport guitarist Richard Thompson, both died instantly. Group members Thompson, Simon Nicol and Tiger Hutchins were all taken to hospital in Stanmore with cuts and bruises. Richard suffered cracked ribs in the crash. Road manager Harvey Bramham was also seriously injured.

Singer Sandy Denny escaped injury because she was not travelling in the group bus. She had made the journey from Birmingham with boyfriend Trevor Lucas, guitarist with Eclection, who had shared the Mother's bill with Fairport Convention on Sunday night.

LAMBLE died instantly

the death crash.

TWO KILLED IN M1 MINI-BUS CRASH

A 27-year-old girl was killed and a young man died of injuries when a mini-bus carrying a pop group careered off the M1 and overturned at Mill today.

Three other youths were injured, two of them seriously.

Their vehicle was involved... man who died was M... ble, a member... Fairport Convention pop group of Radnor Road, Harrow. He died of multiple... after doctors had... two hours to...

The girl... Jeani...

I WAS deeply shocked to learn of the tragic accident in which Martin Lamble died, he will be sadly missed both as a musician and as a person. I hope the other members of the group will recover with great speed and will see fit to continue as a group because I'm sure Martin would have wished it so. — J. COX, London SW7.

WHY FAIRPORT MUST CONTINUE

Fairports a stunning group and beautiful people. I hope they get over this terrible shock and continue to do great things. Good luck, Fairports. — DAVE LANG, Swansea, Glam.

THE UNTIMELY death of ... Lamble of Fairport ... indeed a sad loss to a very excellent yet seriously underated group. I, with many others, hope that this tragedy will not deter the group from continuing to make excellent music and from gaining the recognition that they so truly deserve. — LES DA... Glasgow.

Opposite: The crash, 12 May 1969, in which Martin Lamble and Richard's girlfriend, Jeannie Franklyn, lost their lives

Top: Later in 1969, Fairport hit *Top Of The Pops* with new boys Dave Swarbrick and Dave Mattacks

Below : Pre-performance nerves backstage at the BBC. Left to right: Swarbrick, Thompson, Mattacks, Hutchings, Nicol, Denny

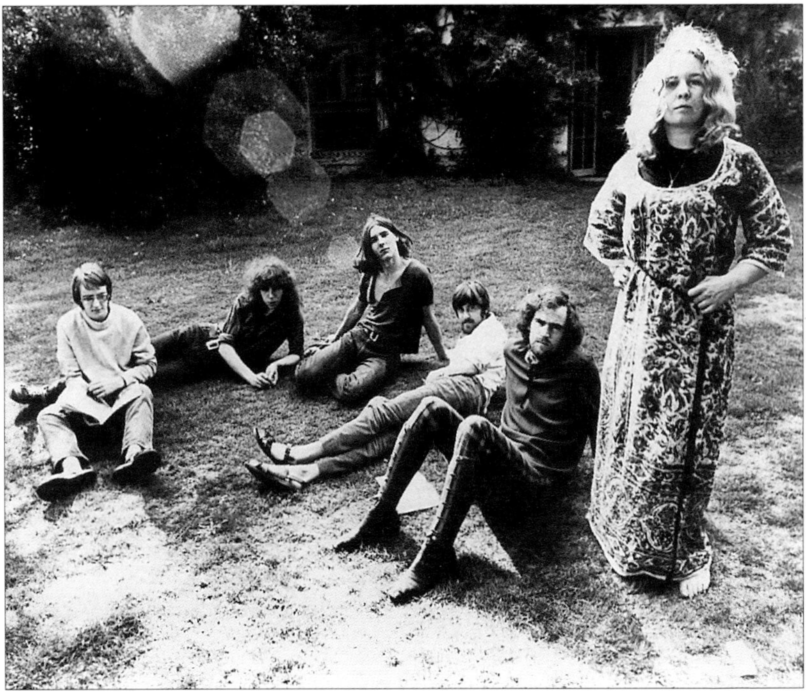

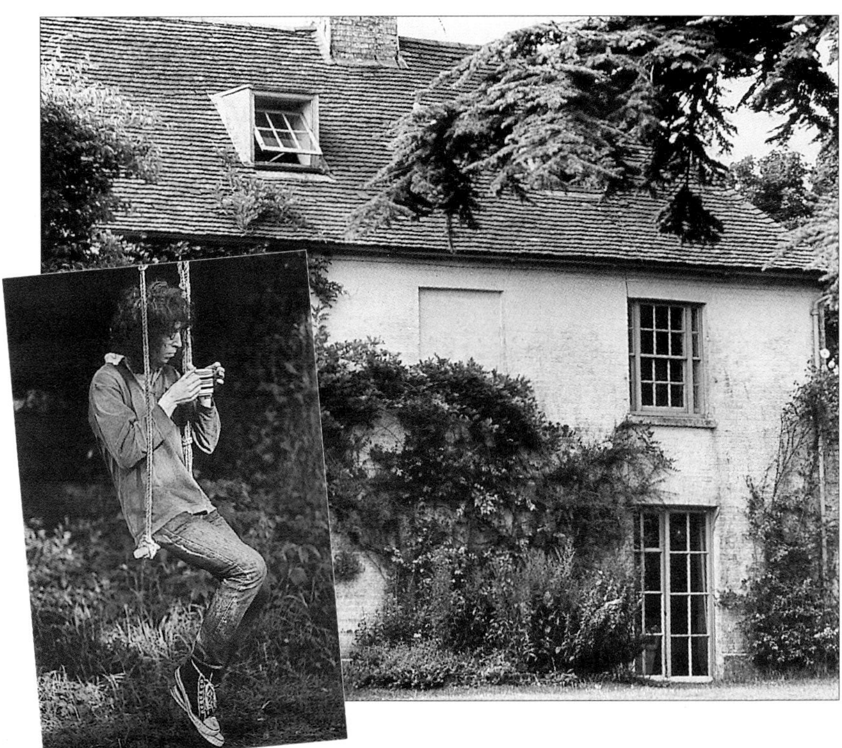

The first (literally) British folk rock LP ever

Liege & Lief
Fairport Convention

ISLAND
ILPS 9115

Documenting a (very brief) era

SANDY DENNY vocals
ASHLEY HUTCHINGS bass guitar
DAVE MATTACKS drums
SIMON NICOL guitars
DAVE SWARBRICK violin, viola
RICHARD THOMPSON guitars

Come All Ye
Reynardine
Matty Groves
Farewell, Farewell
The deserter
Medley: Jigs & Reels
Tam Lin
Crazy Man Michael

PRODUCED BY JOE BOYD
Witchseason Productions Ltd

Opposite top: Fairport relax while creating *Liege & Lief* at Farley Chamberlayne, summer 1969

Opposite below: The Queen Anne mansion in Hampshire where the band lived while rehearsing. Thompson swings!

Above: Full-page ad for the finished album, *Melody Maker* 6 December 1969

Top: The *Full House* line-up, 1970, after Sandy and Ashley split. Fresh-faced new bassist Dave Pegg between Richard and Swarbrick

Above and right: The Angel, a converted pub that became Fairport's new home, and a handbill from late 1970

FREE TRADE HALL
MANCHESTER

FRIDAY, NOV. 6th at 7.45 p.m.

ROY GUEST and VIC LEWIS
present

FAIRPORT CONVENTION
with special guest ROGER RUSKIN SPEAR
AND HIS KINETIC WARDROBE

Tickets: 15/- 13/- 10/- 8/- from Hime and Addison
37 John Dalton Street

When applying for tickets by post, please enclose a stamped self-addressed envelope and cheque or postal order for the correct money. Thanks!

A NEMS PRESENTATION

Primroses' with a Fairport version, what is immediately apparent is that Fairport are simply accentuating the melody already obvious in the song. From there, they developed the fusions apparent on 'A Sailor's Life', the lengthy jam at the end of the song incorporating all manner of musical references outside 'folk'.

Fairport Convention revived, it could be said awoke, interest in a type of music which had previously remained outside the province of a contemporary audience, an audience more attuned to the progressive odysseys undertaken by the bands of the day. But Fairport's strength (partly the reason for their success) was their ability to steer clear of the dry, academic approach, and incorporate, rather than alienate, a potential audience. Fairport were a rock band with a sense of humour, who tackled the *Liege & Lief* project with zealous determination, enthusing over the possibilities, and transmitting their enthusiasm for the traditional music in an invigorating and stimulating manner, thereby awakening an interest in a wider, contemporary audience.

One cannot, of course, make artistic or aesthetic judgements simply on sales figures. But the fact that *Liege & Lief* sold in large quantities indicates that Fairport's experimentation was a success, and from that album alone, many people became aware of their heritage, and bothered to trace it back to source.

Fairport were not simply a band that shoved 400 watts up the backside of a 200-year-old song with an avaricious eye on the Elysian Fields of the Top 10. They were a group fascinated with the possibilities of playing traditional, and more usually unaccompanied, songs with electric instruments. In the process, they actively encouraged their scions to write songs in the folk tradition while maintaining their roots. One thinks particularly of Richard Thompson's success in creating a uniquely *English* form of rock 'n' roll. Their approach helped broaden the boundaries of the folk tradition from which they evolved.

I feel the last word on Fairport's folk rock involvement should come from Ashley Hutchings. He was one of the prime forces in the band to move them wholeheartedly into electric folk, and later went on to form the influential Steeleye Span and the ever-changing Albion Band. When asked about Fairport's contribution, he replied: 'I think they contributed a number of things. We all know that they're the first band to play – to make a success of – British folk rock, we all know that. I'm not saying they were the first band to pick up electric instruments and play folk songs, there might have been a lot of small bands around, and Sweeney's Men certainly tried it. But obviously Fairport were the first to make a success of it, and to form the structure that others would follow. But I also think that an important contribution to music, both folk *and* rock, is the Fairport way of doing things – which is a loose, relaxed, improvised, risk-taking, fun-loving way of setting about making music which, if you actually think about it, isn't how most people, most bands, set about making music.

'We have always been anarchic, and this has continued into the Albions. This way of working, which I learnt with Fairport – which Richard has learnt, and continued with, and Sandy – which is a question of playing with anyone and everyone in a relaxed way, and from that way of working, coming up with new music. Of course, we couldn't have come up with the music if we had been a conventional band. If we had been four guys only, we'd have played a certain type of music in a certain type of venue. We played everything from all over the world at all sorts of venues, and that was what led to *Liege & Lief*. It happened because that's the way we worked. We were willing to take chances!'

5 Come All Ye

At Farley Chamberlayne, Fairport had the run of the house. Their equipment was permanently set up in the big drawing room downstairs, and the group were rehearsing diligently every day. Ashley: 'It was certainly a very magical period, also a very strange period. It wasn't simply us having a ball all the time, there was a lot of heart-searching going on. It was hard work to actually put those things into the rock format, but it was exhilarating and magical in a profound sense.'

Musically, Swarb and Richard were forging a partnership of immense potential, based on their innate musicianship, Swarb's comprehensive knowledge of the folk tradition and Richard's instinctive ability to write in that traditional idiom. Within a couple of months of starting rehearsal, the band were already recording the first fruits of the Swarbrick/Thompson partnership. A week spent in 'darkest Pembrokeshire' (where Swarb lived at the time) for further rehearsal also saw Sandy and Ashley write 'Come All Ye', and the band ready to record.

The actual recording of *Liege & Lief* took place that summer at Sound Techniques (where, incidentally, Richard met Linda Peters for the first time, when she was recording a Kelloggs Cornflakes commercial). Fairport, Joe Boyd and John Wood had now got into a routine about recording – the basic tracks were laid down at Sound Techniques, which was only equipped with 4-

track. From there the tapes went to Olympic Studios, which was equipped with 8-track, for overdubbing, and the final tapes were mixed at Morgan Studios. By now, this being their fourth album, Fairport were a lot more at ease in the studio, and Simon particularly was fascinated by the process of recording (and had received a credit as co-producer of *Unhalfbricking*). Simon: 'We were less awed by the technical apparatus. I got very interested in the production side of things, how it all worked ... Joe would very often sit through an eight-hour session, his feet up on the console, absolutely engrossed in the baseball section of *The New York Herald Tribune* ... He was there as a kind of monitor. If we were barking up the wrong tree he'd come in and say, "Well, I think if maybe you, uh ..." Then he'd go back to the baseball!'

Joe: 'Ultimately it's a producer's job to do whatever is necessary to get the record down, and with them it was always very easy in the studio ... Simon and Richard had very clear ideas about things, and I think that John Wood guided them a lot ... it was a pretty equal and collaborative and very easy, quite pleasant way to produce records. We were all in it together, and everybody had their say. A very egalitarian atmosphere ... we were all coming up with ideas and making suggestions, and we were all having our say about the way things sounded, both I and John Wood the same as everybody else. So it wasn't me standing over them and watching them get on with making the record, it was everybody pitching in with their ideas and suggestions, about the material and the way to do things.'

Although the album was not released until December 1969, the public premiere of the *Liege & Lief* material took place on 20 September at Van Dike's Club in Plymouth. The band's equipment was far from stable throughout the set, and they were all incredibly nervous about how their brand of electric folk would be received.

Simon: 'Everyone was chewing their fingernails to the elbow – those that had any nails left.' But that gig was the first of many triumphs that Fairport achieved on that late summer tour. The rapport between Swarb and Richard meant that the sparks were flying between the two lead instruments, and rock audiences revelled in the novelty of Swarb's electric fiddle pyrotechnics. All this on top of the solid bedrock of Hutchings' bass, Nicol's rhythm guitar and Mattacks' perfectly timed drum patterns. Almost as a bonus, Sandy's flawless vocals rose and soared above the band's swirling electric tapestry.

Not everyone, though, was enchanted by the band's wholehearted commitment to electric folk. Journalist John Platt was one fan who had followed Fairport from the UFO/Middle Earth days and was upset at the speed and fervour with which they espoused their new-found musical direction: 'I think quite a few of their fans would have preferred a *gradual* absorption of traditional material into their set. A lot of people loved the early Fairport. I can remember seeing them at that free concert in Hyde Park in 1968, and being very impressed by the way they handled American material, like "Reno, Nevada" and "Suzanne".'

But Fairport had made their collective mind up, and the Plymouth debut was swiftly followed by a triumphant concert at the Royal Festival Hall on 24 September. The band blasted out their new arrangements of the traditional material through their 400 watt PA, following a nervous Nick Drake and John and Beverly Martyn, who were the opening acts.

That was the gig which divided the folk world into two distinct camps: those who felt that the traditional music was sacrosanct, and should – at the very worst – be accompanied only by an acoustic guitar, and who felt that what Fairport (a self-confessed *rock* band) were attempting was little short of sacrilege. And on the other hand, the more open-minded denizens who – rather like Swarb

Meet On The Ledge

– had become disillusioned with the stultifying attitudes of the folk scene, and who – quite literally – welcomed Fairport's electrifying innovations with open arms. Bert Lloyd was one of the first people to rush up to Sandy after the RFH gig and embrace her, saying that Fairport's set was the most exciting thing he'd heard in years.

In October, Fairport recorded a BBC *Top Gear* session which included an extraordinary version of Cole Porter's 'The Lady Is A Tramp', complete with Frank Sinatra interpretation by Richard Thompson!

Liege & Lief was released just before Christmas 1969, and to date is still Fairport's best-selling album in the UK, with sales exceeding 100,000. It was earmarked for that Valhalla where all the great rock albums go, a crucial album in the history of British rock, ploughing a solitary, adventurous furrow for the legions to follow.

It was with almost single-minded intensity that Fairport had decided to go all the way with *Liege & Lief*, oblivious to the consequences. Ashley: 'If someone had said, "This will do no good to folk music whatsoever, this will do no good to the kids, this will be of no use to anyone other than yourselves", we would still have done it, because that is what we wanted to do! ... It wasn't a formula either, we were playing that way with those instruments because that's what came naturally. We didn't work it out on paper and then think, this could work, let's do it. It's not often said that, I think, because one gets journalists, or other folk musicians, speaking on our behalf and saying, "Well, it's great that you've done this for the music." In all honesty, we didn't do it for the music. We did it for ourselves, and it's great if the music has benefited.'

The album opens with Sandy and Ashley's clarion call, 'Come All Ye', addressed to 'All ye roving minstrels' in an endeavour to 'rouse the spirit of the earth'. A staunch, musical affirmation of Fairport's intentions.

The album's first 'Trad. Arr. Fairport' track comes with

5 Come All Ye

the lovely and mystical 'Reynardine'. The name 'Reynard' is of Dutch derivation, and Reynard the Fox is one of the oldest characters in English myth, drawn upon by Chaucer in *The Canterbury Tales*, and of whom William Caxton wrote *The Historye of reynart the foxe* in 1481. (Fairport's version of 'Reynard The Fox' appeared on their album *Tipplers Tales*.) Fairport's 1969 version of 'Reynardine' is a distillation of the legend, Sandy's clear voice coasting on the splash of cymbals, simply strummed guitar, resonant bass and lightly plucked fiddle.

The following track, 'Matty Groves' became a Fairport 'standard', which surfaced on both their live albums, and was a popular favourite at gigs throughout all subsequent stages of their career. It is an everyday story of love, death and class privilege, narrated over a rousing Fairport backing, marking the first of many classic Swarbrick/Thompson instrumental duets. It is the album's most vigorous reworking of a traditional song (a real folk 'standard'), one which cut right across the board, appealing to both broad-minded purists and rock fans.

The tune for Thompson's 'Farewell, Farewell' comes from the traditional 'Willy O'Winsbury' (culled from the aforementioned influential 1968 *Sweeney's Men* album; Andy Irvine of that band got the text from Child's *English And Scottish Ballads*, but got the numbers jumbled when finding the tune to accompany it and fortuitously came up with the tune which Fairport eventually used). Sandy could not remember the text for the full ballad, so it fell upon Thompson to write fresh words. ('Rotten words, but a great tune,' is how the composer self-effacingly described it to me.)

It is a haunting song of parting, lyrically economic and immeasurably poignant. A classic 'open-road' song: 'The cold north wind will blow again/The winding road does call.' Sandy's rendition leaves the listener in no doubt as to why, for two consecutive years, she won the *Melody Maker* 'Best British Female Singer' award.

'The Deserter' gives a harrowing picture of mid-19th-century Army life, the song's central character being saved only by royal intervention. Ratcliffe Highway, in London's East End, was a notorious haunt of criminals and deserters in the aftermath of the Napoleonic Wars.

The reels and jigs were (are) a popular favourite at all Fairport gigs, a splendid opportunity for a virtuoso Swarb performance. Of all the traditional songs which Fairport chose for the album, probably the richest in terms of imagery is 'Tam Lin', a mystical excursion into the taboo grounds of Carterhaugh, rich in fairies, elves and milk-white steeds. The imagery found favour with those still delighting in the Middle Earth of Tolkien. Fairport's version of the song is drawn from a text attributed to Robert Burns.

The first intimation of the powers of the vintage Swarbrick/Thompson combination came on the album's final track, 'Crazy Man Michael'; Swarbrick already had the tune, and Thompson added the words separately. At the heart of the song is its wonderful elemental imagery: Michael striking at the four winds with his fists, ranting and raving to the night and the day in the penultimate verse, when we learn that it is the raven who is the 'true love' that he has destroyed. It reads particularly well too, notably the final verse, with Michael now a 'Wandering Jew' character, forever 'the Keeper of the Garden'.

One tends to agree with Ashley Hutchings when he talks about that album: 'If you look at the *Liege & Lief* cover, that gives a very good idea of the feeling. There's a lot of magic on that cover, and that's the way I feel about it. I think it was blessed. I think all that union was blessed.'

But Richard Thompson has less fond memories of the album: 'I prefer *Unhalfbricking* ... *Liege & Lief* sounds slightly artificial, too claustrophobic, over-arranged. There was a dimension missing – it needed more space in the music.' The British music press were delighted with Fairport's achievements on *Liege & Lief*, but *Rolling Stone* in its review of 'Leif And Leige' [*sic*] was not impressed. Although conceding 'that the bass of Mr Hutchings and the drums of Mr Mattacks rescue it from dire Pentanglish sterile folkiness' it petulantly asked 'Where, essentially, is something to excite those of us who find artiness worthy enough of quiet admiration, but a little boring?'

In a 1974 interview, quoted in *The Electric Muse*, Swarb captured the excitement of that period: 'You know, if you're singing about a bloke having his head chopped off, or a girl fucking her brother and having a baby, and the brother getting pissed off and cutting her guts open and stamping on the baby and killing his sister – now that's a fantastic story by any standards, whether told in a pub or on Broadway. Having to work with a storyline like that with acoustic instruments wouldn't be half as potent dramatically as saying the same things electrically.'

Simon reflected more philosophically, but just as enthusiastically, in a 1969 *Disc* interview about what Fairport were attempting to achieve on *Liege & Lief*: 'When it comes down to folk, it's still a form of music that's very alive, but has always been restricted. The songs exist in libraries and in folk clubs, but the people who play in folk clubs, and the people who go to listen, never advance. It's always been the same people singing the same songs to the same audience. A kind of innate snobbery . . . I'm sure the kids are completely unaware of their heritage. I count myself among the kids, because I was reared on music that was always a distillation of American influences. We feel the time is right to bring the music out – getting away from the blues scale and introducing something completely new. All the folk songs have reached a very pure form by now – a kind of sorting the wheat from the chaff. And there are some fantastic songs about. I mean, there's nothing like a good murder ballad to get them going!'

The challenge and stimulation which *Liege & Lief* offered Fairport Convention occupied them in the months after the crash. They had recently scored a Top 30 single (and however unrepresentative it may have been, it helped bring their name to a wider audience), and the initial critical and commercial success of the project found them – at least for the time being – unified. The possibilities seemed limitless, clearly suggesting the path they and their disciples could pursue.

6 Walk Awhile

Even before *Liege & Lief* was in the shops, two more departures split Fairport, which threatened the band's very existence. Founder member Ashley Hutchings and Sandy Denny – who, for many, *was* Fairport Convention – left within days of each other in November 1969.

Musical differences, personal problems and factions within the band were all contributory factors to the split. Richard: 'Around that time I had the feeling there were so many people in the band, too many strong personalities. We all tended to pare off . . .'

Sandy was clearly unhappy that the band, driven by Ashley and Swarbrick, was to continue the course ordained by *Liege & Lief*, which was an album that she regarded as a one-off experiment. However successful and influential it may have been, Sandy was keen to develop her own writing, which was something Ashley was not in favour of encouraging, at least not within the context of Fairport Convention.

Sandy was the first to actually leave. Fairport were due in Copenhagen to record a TV show and gig there for a week. When the car called at Sandy and Trevor's flat to collect her, Sandy wasn't there. The band had been working at Mother's in Birmingham the night before, and Simon had come down with Sandy on the last train to London. Simon: 'She spent most of the journey in tears, about how she loved the band, and how she loved Trevor so much. How she didn't want to go to America, how she didn't even want to go to Denmark for a week... Sandy was a person who needed a lot of affection and attention. She could see the band getting bigger, and we were talking about going to the States for the first time. She got the horrors about being separated from Trevor for a long period.'

Anthea Joseph of Witchseason eventually tracked Sandy down at Trevor's sister's flat in Holland Park, and flew with her to Denmark to join up with the rest of the band. Simon: 'On the way to the airport in the car, the four of us talked about the future. Ashley was as positive as anyone, and it was at that time, between Fulham and the airport, that Ashley suggested Bert Lloyd join, which was a concept I couldn't cope with, and I think the others found it hard to cope with.'

The fact that, as Simon says, Ashley was 'as positive as anyone', indicated that leaving the band was far from clear in his mind. He was personally delighted with the results of – and the opportunities afforded by – *Liege & Lief*. Following his discussions with Tim Hart, Gay and Terry Woods and Maddy Prior at the Keele Folk Festival earlier in the year about developing the possibilities of electric folk, he had a clear idea in his head about the direction he wished Fairport Convention to pursue.

Ashley: 'During the trip over to Denmark, we talked about the future, as well as the current situation ... and it threw up quite a lot of things about the future ... I think I had made up my mind that it was going to go a certain way, and that Sandy – who was agitating to make *Liege & Lief* a one-off project – maybe would not be in the band in the future, and that we would get a traditional singer in and push it further that way ... All these thoughts were going on in my head, and when we arrived in Copenhagen, we had a telephone call to say that Sandy would be on the next plane ... And I had a strange reaction to this, which I wasn't in total control of, and I think I decided within a day or two of that happening that I was going to leave the band.'

Joe Boyd, although still ostensibly Fairport's manager and record producer, only really came into contact with them in the studio, as the management side was handled by his Witchseason company. Knowing them as he did, Boyd can lend objectivity to an analysis of the band's convolutions. Joe: 'They decided that that particular direction which they had been going in – as a kind of English answer to American folk rock – was what they were going to become, a truly English band, concentrating on British material. I think this was a combination of Richard's feelings, Sandy's interests and the new-found conversion of Ashley . . . I remember they spoke to Swarbrick, and were quite delighted to discover he was as interested with the experiment as they had been, and that he would contemplate joining.

'Sandy's feelings about that were not quite as rational. She had been involved with the traditional for a long time, but always rather ambivalently. She sang traditional songs as well as her own compositions, and she had two feelings about it. One was a kind of amusement at Ashley's fanaticism, which he came to very late in life. He was discovering things with the zeal of a new convert that she had been familiar with . . . for years. She had been singing songs that he would come back from Cecil Sharp House with and say, "I have just discovered this magnificent song." And she would say, "Well, I was singing that when I was 17!" I also think that Sandy's career in the folk scene suffered a bit at the hands of the purists, who always viewed her as a corrupter. She sang with a guitar, she didn't sing unaccompanied, she sang her own compositions, which at that time was considered a little "Not Done" in the traditional circuit. In a way, joining Fairport had been her step away from it all into a different world.

Meet On The Ledge

'To suddenly discover that, having gotten into the rock 'n' roll business, she was now in the same band as someone who was fast becoming almost as doctrinaire about British traditional music as all those people she had fled folk from . . .! I think that was a little traumatic for her, and also Ashley's point of view that her songs – or Richard's songs for that matter – were not really to be encouraged. That this was not going to be a group that was going to sing the songs of their two leading songwriters, that they were going to be scouring the archives for traditional material, this, I think, alarmed her as well.'

Ashley: 'There wasn't any animosity towards Sandy, who was always a friend, but there was a slightly let-down feeling of "here we go again, we're going to turn the clock back". When my hopes were raised that we were going to take a leap into a new direction with maybe a new singer . . . It was just a feeling of desperately wanting to pursue that can of beans we had opened, and Sandy was particularly against that.'

Of all ex-Fairporters, Ashley Hutchings has probably led the most interesting and varied career(s) and has stayed true to the ideals he developed, and which he wanted Fairport to pursue at the time of *Liege & Lief*. Within weeks of leaving Fairport, he was in the process of forming the band he saw as a vehicle for performing traditional English folk music utilising electric instruments. The result was Steeleye Span, with whom Hutchings stayed for three albums, eventually persuading Martin Carthy to plug in and join them. It was with Steeleye that Ashley got the taste for theatre work – they worked with playwright Keith Dewhurst on a number of productions at London's Royal Court Theatre.

Steeleye, of course, went on to considerable commercial success, but Hutchings left them in 1971, and became immersed in the Albion Country Band, which involved Ashley and his (then) wife Shirley Collins, with a floating personnel. The 'beetle-browed' Hutchings then formed the Albion Dance Band (which, as its name suggests, was formed specifically for dance purposes), which metamorphosed into the Albion Band.

The Albion Band is a flexible organisation which recorded a number of excellent albums (notably *Rise Up Like the Sun* in 1977, which reunited Hutchings with former Fairport producer Joe Boyd). They also provided memorable scores for a number of National Theatre productions, like *The Passion* and *Lark Rise*. Hutchings was also the prime force behind the Albions' *River Hymn*, which was a history of the Thames in music and prose, drawn effectively from the works of Charles Dickens, Lewis Carroll and Spike Milligan.

The popular image of Ashley Hutchings is of a zealous academic as far as traditional music is concerned, treating it as reverentially as the traditionalists he had so offended with Fairport. But his ears are as open to contemporary music and musicians as ever. (It was he who suggested the effective use of Dylan's 'When The Ship Comes In' during the Noah's Ark scene in *The Passion*.) His choice of musicians for the Albion Band was always astute and imaginative, and his 'Albion Band Source Nights' gave a fascinating insight into the creative processes and influences which helped shape that most malleable of bands.

Ashley Hutchings has been responsible for organising some of the best nights of music I have ever seen, and I am sure that whichever path his Muse leads him down, it will be a rich and rewarding one for an audience to follow.

Fairport Convention, meanwhile, were left riding high on a wave of popular and critical success, but minus their influential bass player and singer – at the end of a year marred by the tragedy of the crash, but fired with musical purpose and conviction.

It looked like being the end for a band that – during its

short two-year career – had achieved so much, and for whom so much more seemed possible. But Fairport Convention were possessed of a resilience which astounded their critics and fans, and amazed even the band themselves.

Of paramount importance to them was finding the right bass player to replace Ashley. Both Nicol and Thompson considered switching to bass, but it was decided that, realistically, a new member was essential. On Swarbrick's insistence, the band auditioned his fellow Brummie Dave Pegg. It was a move which Joe Boyd called 'one of the single most important things to have happened to Fairport Convention'.

Peggy's audition for Fairport was his second that day. In the morning he had tried out for the Foundations ('The original 2-Tone band,' mused Simon), and he came down to the Fairport audition in the afternoon.

Simon: 'Swarb was pretty definite about this guy's pedigree, said he plays great bass and mandolin, and is a great bloke . . .'

Peggy's musical background was that of the flourishing Birmingham beat scene of the mid-sixties, which produced the Move, half of Led Zeppelin, Steve Winwood, Roy Wood, ELO and many more. Dave Pegg was born in November 1947 and attended the Yardley Grammar School, where Ian Campbell had been a pupil some years before. According to Peggy, the 'King Cat' at Yardley was Brian Hynes (later known as Denny Laine, of the Moody Blues and Wings), and the main school band was Denny Laine And The Diplomats, which also featured ELO's Bev Bevan on drums.

The Shadows were the guvnor group of the time, and Peggy persuaded his father to buy him a guitar, so he could emulate good old Hank, and it was as a guitarist that he spent his formative years playing with various semi-pro Brum bands.

6 Walk Awhile

On leaving school he worked as a clerk with the Royal Exchange Insurance Company, and in the evenings played guitar with the Crawdaddys, who frequently supported major Brum bands like the Spencer Davis Group and the Moody Blues. The Roy Everett Blues Band was his next step, still on guitar, then on to the Ugleys, a pop band who covered Byrds and Dylan material in the flourishing Brum scene of 1965/66. (The cross-referencing of band members and choice of material was very similar to the North London welter of Fairport around this time.) The Ugleys featured Steve Gibbons on vocals and Roger Hill on guitar, who later appeared in a Fairport connection in 1972. It was because of Hill's prowess as a guitarist that Peggy decided to switch to bass.

The Ugleys actually managed to land a small record deal, and one single Peggy definitely remembers playing on was a Ray Davies song 'End Of The Season', which never achieved anything here, but was apparently a minor hit in Australia. Peggy looked back on those days with great affection: 'Every big pub would have a dance on . . . You'd get fifteen quid, chip in a couple of quid for petrol, stick maybe four quid in your pocket and get drunk for a quid, so it was paradise.'

The Exception was his next step, a blues trio with Peggy on bass, Roger Hill on guitar and one Alan Eastwood on vocals. They cut a couple of singles, which flopped, although 'The Eagle Flies on Friday' did feature Robert Plant on tambourine. The Zeppelin connection was further consolidated with Peggy's next band, The Way Of Life, featuring two brothers, Chris and Reg Jones, with John Bonham on drums. They only played about 30 gigs. Bonham went on to join Led Zeppelin, and Peggy switched to stand-up bass for a spell with the Ian Campbell Folk Group. He stayed there for just over a year, learning mandolin in the process and acquiring a love for traditional folk music, as well as making many useful contacts on the contemporary folk circuit, such as Swarb and Ralph McTell, with whom he worked in later years. But towards the end of 1968 and beginning of 1969, the 'progressive' movement was fully under way, and Peggy was itching to get back to playing electric bass.

He left the Campbells, and along with Cozy Powell (later of Jeff Beck's group and Rainbow) and Dave Clempson, formed the Beast, which rehearsed for two months before Clempson left to join Jon Hiseman's Colosseum. Fairport came into Peggy's life on his 21st birthday: 'Fairport were playing Mother's in Birmingham. Sandy and Tyger were still with them, and we went along with Harvey Andrews, who was a mate of ours, and he hated it, but I loved it.

'They didn't play in Brum that much, and I'd been involved in the folk scene a bit, and thought, this is great, I'd love to join that band, *and* it was my 21st birthday. Then the next week I got the call from Swarb saying, "Tyger's left, will you come along?" '

Joe: 'I think the band were beginning to figure out the phrasing and wording for an ad in *MM*, or ... ringing bass players, and Swarbrick kept telling them that he knew this guy in Birmingham who was a great bass player. They still had this feeling about Swarbrick, that he was a folkie, and they cross-examined him about this guy. Swarb said he used to play stand-up bass with the Ian Campbell Folk Group, and they rolled their eyes a little bit, said "great", and immediately dismissed the idea. I don't think they took it very seriously, and thought that Swarbrick obviously didn't know what a good rock 'n' roll bass player needs to be. They were determined to get somebody who was as solid as a rock, who could really play bass, but Swarbrick refused to shut up about this guy – how he could get him down from Birmingham and they could meet him. So ultimately, as a kind of indulgence to Swarbrick, just to shut him up ... because they *knew* this guy would not be suitable, they agreed to try him out.

6 **Walk Awhile**

'We walked into this little basement room in Kennington, and they were playing "Tam Lin", or "Matty Groves", and Pegg was playing all those incredibly difficult bass lines Ashley had invented. All those bass lines were great, Ashley invented them all, but he never could play them that well. He thought of them, but he was technically not a terrific bass player. He was a very inventive, melodic bass player, but not a very powerful one technically. But having had the part explained to him once, Pegg was playing it better than Ashley ever played it.

'Simon and Richard were just staring at this guy across the room, and trying to concentrate on playing the guitar while watching this amazing performance. I think Swarbrick had probably coached him a bit before, and maybe told him to listen to the records and learn the parts. But to me that was the key event, because Pegg, in a way, is the biggest difference.

'In some rock bands, I think, ultimately, the bands that sound great, you can generally trace it to the bass player. It's a most important element really. It was at that point they became a great band, when they had Pegg. It was perfect, because it couldn't have happened without Ashley's inventiveness and his definition of that style of bass playing that the group needed.'

Fairport welcomed Peggy with open arms. He has an affable, engaging personality, and has proved over his years with the band just how astute Joe Boyd's original judgement was. Within weeks, Swarb's idea of getting Peggy into the band had been vindicated.

Simon: 'DM took to Peggy immediately, the timekeeping thing, a rhythmic understanding... DM was really up for keeping the band going; the Palais bands he'd come from were just somewhere to pick up birds, and beat people up to the background of tasteful music... Swarb kept the ball rolling, he'd got the bit between his teeth. He wasn't going to let the band fold.'

Fairport were emphatic that they were not going to look for a replacement for Sandy. Her short spell with the band had made such an impression that it would have been a thankless task to find anyone capable of filling the void she left. The 'English Jefferson Airplane' tag was a long way behind them by then, and Fairport did not feel behoven to find a replacement female singer.

With Peggy recruited, it was decided that they should find a place where the whole band could live and rehearse. Swarb was living in Milford Haven, which was extremely inconvenient for recording and gigging, Simon and his wife Roberta had a flat in London, Peggy and his wife were in Brum, and Richard was still at the old Brent flat (where his favourite listening was BBC sound effects records of steam trains!).

At the bitter end of 1969, Simon and Robin Gee (who was then employed by Witchseason, after a spell with Family, and who had been 'a strong, supportive factor' when Ashley and Sandy left) went house-hunting for Fairport. One of the places they looked at was an old Ind Coope pub – the Angel – in Little Hadham, near Bishop's Stortford, which Simon thought was 'a total waste of time; it was empty, cold and damp'. The two drove back to London, only to receive a call on their return to the Witchseason offices from Swarb, to say that he had arrived with his wife and daughter and moved into the pub!

The Angel played a substantial part in the corporate life of Fairport Convention for the next two years. Eventually Simon and his wife, Richard, Peggy and his family, DM and wife, Swarb and family, Robin Gee and his wife were all living there.

Although no longer in use as a pub, a plan seriously considered by the band at one stage was to commission the brilliant cartoonist Bill Tidy to design a fresh pub sign for the Angel, to be renamed 'The Clog and Bells', as all the band were fans of his Cloggies strip in *Private Eye*.

6 Walk Awhile

It was there at the beginning of 1970 that the five-man Fairport began rehearsing for their forthcoming gigs. It was an enormous place, so the equipment could be permanently set up, and the band were free to wander in and out and rehearse in their own time, even if the sanitary arrangements left a lot to be desired! It was at the Angel that Richard and Swarb wrote the material which appeared on *Full House*, round the big open fire downstairs after everyone else had retired.

Simon: 'Swarb and Richard's writing was a side effect of the band living together ... there was a certain kind of unlikely magic. They could produce spontaneous music in the studio, which is jolly difficult ... To be able to do the sort of thing they refined on "Sloth" is not really something you can work at. Ninety per cent has to be there, even before you meet.'

In a 1981 *MM* interview, Swarb viewed that period quite differently: 'Richard and I never got on in the early days of FC ... we thought we did, but we never did. We composed some bloody good songs together, but it was purely on a basis of "you write that and I'll write this, and we'll put it together". But we never sat down and had real good chats.'

Dave Pegg's debut with the band was at the Country Club in Hampstead on 29 January 1970. Peggy: 'We were rehearsing for a month, and it was the pre-gig rehearsal ... I was a gibbering lunatic; *I* couldn't sing, I could hardly talk ... nobody was singing. I had a list of all the numbers, what key they were in, so I had my bit together. But I thought, they can't *all* be instrumentals, so they tossed a coin to see who was going to sing, and it was down to Swarb and Richard!'

Richard: 'There were five good people, all jolly good pals, good chemistry ... I think everyone could sing, but we all lacked confidence. I think, really, we should have had a singer in.'

The lack of a clearly defined vocalist in the *Full House* days was a problem which affected Fairport considerably during those years, but despite the band's lack of confidence, they were well received on that tour. There was a reunion of sorts in April, when Fairport played the 'Pop Proms' at the Roundhouse, along with Matthews Southern Comfort and Fotheringay. Of that gig, Richard Williams wrote in *The Times*: 'They are, in fact, currently presenting the most promising avenue for pop progression in this country.'

It was also in April that Fairport Convention made their long-overdue American debut. They toured with Jethro Tull, and supported such luminaries as Traffic at the Fillmore, and Crosby, Stills, Nash and Young at Winterland. But the highlight of the tour was their week-long residency, supporting Rick Nelson and the Stone Canyon Band, at the Troubadour in Los Angeles. (The fruits of that week became apparent seven years later with the release of *Live At The LA Troubadour*.) According to Peggy, the whole band received 500 dollars for the five nights, but had unlimited access to the house bar. Fairport ended up owing the Troubadour 1500 dollars! He and Swarb were also refused entry to Disneyland because of their scruffy appearance.

Fairport attracted a good deal of attention, and a number of celebrities came down to see them play, including Odetta, Maria Muldaur, Linda Ronstadt (who joined them on stage for a version of 'Silver Threads And Golden Needles') and Led Zeppelin.

Zeppelin were, of course, old mates of Peggy's from Brum, and were playing to capacity audiences at the Forum in LA, and after their set there, came down to the Troubadour 'for a knock'. Richard was playing a Gibson Les Paul, and Simon was playing a semi-acoustic guitar with very heavy strings, which Jimmy Page played, remarking afterwards that 'it was like trying to play railway lines'. DM had to claim a new drum kit after Bonham had finished playing it. The Mobile was there to record the live album, and quick thinking on the part of someone from the Fairport camp meant that a three-hour tape exists somewhere of Fairport Convention jamming with Led Zeppelin on old rock 'n' roll standards and some frantic jigs and reels, where Page, apparently, had great difficulty in keeping up with Thompson!

Simon described the audience reaction to Fairport in the States as 'warm, but puzzled'. The Troubador also introduced Fairport to another aspect of American live performance – more than one show a night. They played two sets a night during the week, and three on the weekends, which was no strain for Mattacks, who was quite used to it from his days with the Palais bands. Fairport gigged extensively in the States during the two months they were there, and also recorded the vocal tracks for *Full House* ('whoever happened to be in the studio,' according to Peggy). Two days were spent recording at Gold Star Studios in LA, where Fairport tried a version of 'The Bonny Bunch Of Roses' with Richard singing, but it didn't turn out to their satisfaction, and it was scrapped. It was to be a further seven years before they felt confident enough to record it.

On their return to Britain, Fairport played the enormous Bath Festival at the end of June. An estimated 300,000 people went along to hear Led Zeppelin, Jefferson Airplane, Pink Floyd (who premiered *Atom Heart Mother* at 3 a.m.) and Santana. Swarb and Peggy almost didn't make it at all, getting stuck in the enormous traffic jams which clogged all the roads to the Shepton Mallet site, and it was only by cadging lifts off a couple of Hell's Angels that they managed to make the gig. Although scheduled to appear at 2 p.m. on the Saturday afternoon, they didn't get on stage until six, and the following morning they were off to a gig in Rotterdam. In early July they played a benefit for the St Cecilia's church organ fund in Little Hadham, which raised £450, and helped ensure a victory for Miss Caroline Shillacker in the ankle competition!

In between these diverse gigs, Fairport managed to get down and record their crucial fifth album, *Full House*, their first without a female singer, and one on which the vocal problem had still to be resolved. Joe Boyd felt that Swarbrick was keen to do more singing, and was able to convince Richard that he (Richard) should tackle more lead singing. Ironically, it was the usually reticent Simon Nicol whose voice is the first you hear on the opening track, 'Walk Awhile', the first of three classic Swarbrick/Thompson songs on the album. Thompson is typically self-effacing about these songs: 'Really, I think, we were driven by boredom and a need for material for the album.' Thompson's sleeve notes for the album attracted a great deal of attention at the time, a surrealistic continuation of the academic notes which embellished *Liege & Lief*, inspired more by Flann O'Brien than Lewis Carroll. Although 'The Jolly Hangman' is featured prominently on the sleeve notes, the song 'Poor Will And The Jolly Hangman', which had been recorded for the album, did not appear on the final version, for reasons which are explained later.

Full House marks the zenith of the short-lived Swarbrick/Thompson partnership, and is my favourite Fairport album. It is an album which offers the band ample opportunity to display their instrumental dexterity on two lengthy traditional instrumentals, shows how fully Peggy had integrated, offers Swarbrick and Thompson on vintage form and has a full, rich sound courtesy of Messrs Boyd and Wood. Any vocal deficiencies are ably covered by 'les toutes ensembles'.

'Walk Awhile' is a deceptively jaunty opening track, implying an album of fun and frolics to follow, whereas the overall theme of *Full House* lies on the side of resigned doom, affirming Thompson's jaundiced view of humanity. However breezy 'Walk Awhile' may sound, lines like 'Undertakers bow their heads as you go passing by' are indicative of the despondency never far below the surface. More characteristic is the gloomily magnificent 'Doctor Of Physick', a moral tale, which *Rolling Stone* likened to 'a giant tarantula'. A song full of unnamed menace, made all the more eerie by the sparsely ominous chorus of 'Doctor Monk unpacks his trunk tonight', hinting at all manner of necromancy contained within the trunk and implying that the Hippocratic Oath had long since been forgotten by the good doctor! It was proof positive of Swarbrick and Thompson's ability to convincingly assimilate the traditional 'feel', from the sage, parental advice proferred concerning the loss of maidenhead, to the line 'wear your relic near', which suggests age-old superstition, man's desire to clasp relics to ward off the evil lurking in the dark beyond the cottage door.

The traditional 'Sir Patrick Spens' is pared down to a basic nine-verse narrative, driven forcibly along by the band, the vocals spread between the four front men (there is also a lovely version of the song in the BBC archives from 1969, with Sandy singing).

'Flowers Of The Forest' is a lilting Scottish lament, enhanced by Mattacks' sombre drums and Nicol's lovely sounding dulcimer. It is one of the most beautiful Scottish laments, and was played by a solitary piper at the funerals of both Sandy and Phil Ochs.

But the album's zenith – and the song which, to my mind, is the highlight of the Swarbrick/Thompson collaboration – is 'Sloth', the near ten-minute epic which wraps up side one. Lyrically, reproduced on the printed page, its sparsity belies its epic qualities. An evocative tale of war, death, love and parting, it is a chilling glimpse through a tiny keyhole into a world where 'The right thing's the wrong thing', where definitions of 'good' and 'bad' are blurred and indistinct. Where the warring factions are never still, corroding dignity in an atmosphere of melancholic resignation.

The lyrical leanness by implication suggests something far more majestic and profound, and the line quoted previously brings to mind the W. B. Yeats poem 'The Second Coming': 'The best lack all conviction, while the worst are full of passionate intensity.'

Thompson's subdued interjection of 'She's run away, she's run away, and she ran so bitterly' followed by Swarb's achingly restrained fiddle break, implies a far deeper meaning than the scant four lines actually state. A framework for something deeper, suggesting a complex narrative, the novel that Thomas Hardy always *meant* to write.

The band play with a brooding passion, softly strummed guitars over Mattacks' precise drumming and Peggy's resonant bass, and Swarbrick's fiddle playing is at its most deft and atmospheric throughout. The plaintive chorus at the song's conclusion, 'Just a roll, just a roll', is a moving climax to a great song.

The critics were united in proclaiming the success of the reborn Fairport and the achievement of *Full House*. *Rolling Stone* called it 'a triumph'. *NME*'s Nick Logan called the album 'Brilliant . . . exciting . . . It could well be their finest album to date.' *Record Mirror* said that Fairport 'have done for British folk music what bands such as the Flying Burrito Brothers, the Byrds, or even Bob Dylan have done for American country music'.

Tony Palmer in the *Observer* called the album: 'A triumphant return . . . They embody the best elements of what has come to be known as folk rock . . . They have used the weapons of rock music, its excitement, its sense of occasion, its pounding fascination, to enrich and revitalise the popular music of the past.' Karl Dallas, in his review in *The Times*, made a number of acute observations, comparing Fairport to the approach of American dramatist Charles Marowitz, in the way he reworked *Hamlet* and *Macbeth*: 'Fairport Convention replace reverence with passionate involvement, restating the contemporary meaning of the ancient stories.'

During their period together, the *Full House* line-up produced only one album, and an original single which is available on the 1972 *History Of ...* album. 'Now Be Thankful' was written by Swarb and Richard in Boston during their American tour. The B-side is best remembered for the longest title of any song ever commercially released, although it did turn up, in abbreviated form, on the 1974 live album: 'Sir B. Mackenzie's Daughter's Lament For The 77th Mounted Lancers Retreat From The Straights Of Loch Knombe On The Occasion Of The Announcement Of Her Marriage To The Laird of Kinleakie'! Swarbrick remembers the band having little idea of how the song would actually turn out, and shouting instructions to each other across the studio while they were recording. 'When it was recorded, we thought we might as well aim for *The Guinness Book Of Records* with the title.'

Although not issued until seven years later, the tapes of *Live At The LA Troubadour* were with Island, culled from the band's residency there in 1970. Joe Boyd calls the delay: 'A sore point ... I always liked it, and I very much wanted to have it out ... but they were more concerned in getting *Full House* out ... I left and went to America, and Richard left the group, and it became Swarbrick's group, and eventually Trevor joined, and then Sandy came in, and always this album was something that represented the old group. I kept pestering Island to put it out and, essentially, as long as the group was signed to Island ... they felt the determination of what came out should be the group's.' Swarbrick in particular was far from happy with the quality of the tapes, and campaigned against their issue, but eventually relented.

Live At The LA Troubadour is of interest for a number of reasons. It displays the *Full House* line-up live, at their unequivocal best, and contains another gem from the Swarbrick/Thompson days. Joe Boyd felt 'Poor Will And The Jolly Hangman' should have been included on *Full House*, but Thompson stubbornly refused, claiming he was unhappy with his solo. Joe: 'I felt the album (*Full House*) lacked enough minutes on it. I think it ended up being 18/19 minutes a side, and with "Poor Will" it was going to be 20/21 minutes a side . . . But I just felt in terms of balance it was part of the mood of the album.'

The song did eventually materialise, first on *The Electric Muse* four-album set, then on Richard's *Guitar, Vocal*, by which time he had presumably come to terms with his solo. The version on *Guitar, Vocal* is, in fact, the same version recorded by Fairport and featured on the *Troubadour* album; for *Guitar, Vocal* their backing vocals were simply removed and replaced by Linda's. 'Poor Will' is another example of that rich Swarbrick/Thompson collaboration, further displaying Thompson's jaundiced, world-weary style, with the finely ironic chorus of 'Here's a toast to the jolly hangman/He'll hang you the best that he can', his mournful vocals conjuring up graphic images of Judge Jeffreys, Tyburn Tree and a capacity crowd.

That atmosphere was one which Greil Marcus captured in his 1977 piece on Fairport in *The Village Voice*: 'Thompson, however, was straight out of the Plague years. One imagines him following behind a cart full of corpses, strumming a lute, laughing at the stupidity of man's faith, cursing God with his next breath.'

Linda Thompson spoke to me once about her husband's reputation as a writer who constantly dwells on the gloomier side of the human condition: 'He's terribly capable of songs of the moment. You know, you'll get a very transitory mood of total despair or total euphoria, and he's very capable of transcribing that. And then it goes, because things are never *that* bad.'

Musically, the album is a strong testament to the Fairport of that period – the two lengthy work-outs on 'Matty Groves' and 'Sloth' demonstrate the band firing on all cylinders. Thompson's doleful vocal on 'Matty Groves' is in many ways preferable to the *Liege & Lief* version. Swarb's frantic fiddling on 'Mason's Apron' is fast enough (in the words of David Hepworth, whose sleeve notes to the *Troubadour* album are both amusing and perceptive, capturing the album's feel perfectly) 'to knacker a whirling Dervish'! It is one of the few occasions where speed triumphs over actual musical ability, leaving the listener counting his own digits. Peggy's bass lines are a delight, and listening to the album it is hard to believe he had been in the band for only a few months, such is his empathy with Mattacks.

Troubadour is by no means a perfect album, but it is a fascinating and all too rare example of the *Full House* line-up at work. The muted audience applause can only be attributed to the bemused Rick Nelson fans confronted by an English band way beyond their ken. 'Hello Mary Lou' was never like this!

The *Full House/Troubadour* period was the last time Joe Boyd was to work with Fairport, the band he had done so much to help. An offer from Warner Brothers in America came when he was at a particularly low point ('probably nothing a three-month holiday wouldn't have cured').

Boyd was having problems with the artists he was closely involved with, and the period marked the nadir of his relationship with Thompson. Joe: 'My primary interest in Fairport Convention was in Richard ... It was Richard's group, insofar as there was any taking of sides, or arbitrating of disputes to be done ... I would try gently to push the group in the direction of what Richard wanted to do ... because I thought that his instincts were always the best ... Richard was becoming more perverse in the studio. We had a lot of arguments over *Full House* ... He was very fussy about things, and whenever I said, "I like that solo, let's keep it," he would say, "No, erase, I want to do another." And whenever I said, "No, I don't like that, let's do another one," he would say, "No, I like it, let's keep it"!'

Mike Heron of the Incredible String Band was becoming more immersed in Scientology, Nick Drake was emphatic that his next album would be just him and guitar, Sandy and Fotheringay were causing Boyd managerial problems, and he wasn't seeing eye to eye with Thompson. Joe: 'Sandy, Nick, Richard and Mike were the four that were my main concern in life. It seemed to me that they weren't too interested in listening to my advice, and I was finding it more difficult to work with all of them.'

So Boyd accepted Warners' offer, and worked with them on the Jimi Hendrix documentary and the soundtracks for *A Clockwork Orange* and *Deliverance* before returning to record production work in the mid-seventies. He produced the charming debut album of Kate and Anna McGarrigle and worked on their subsequent albums, produced three albums for Maria Muldaur and one for Toots And The Maytals, before being happily reunited with Ashley Hutchings on the Albions' *Rise Up Like The Sun* in 1977: 'After I left, of all the Fairport people, what Ashley did was the most interesting and adventurous, much to my surprise.' Of all the Fairport albums he was involved in, Joe Boyd cites *Unhalfbricking* as his favourite: 'I can put it on and just listen to it without thinking, why didn't I mix that differently, or why wasn't this tune included, or I wish I had won that argument with Richard about that solo, or something ... *Unhalfbricking* is just a seamless album as far as I'm concerned.'

6 Walk Awhile

Fairport Convention had decided – despite their own uncertainty about their vocal prowess – to pursue the electric folk route, and encourage the blossoming Swarbrick/Thompson partnership. *Full House* had certainly been an affirmation of the wisdom of their decision, the best of both worlds. They steered clear of an academic approach with their traditional interpretations.

In an interview with Bob Pegg in an August 1970 issue of *Zig Zag*, Richard confessed: 'I really think that if I understood traditional music, I wouldn't be playing electric guitar.' And Linda Thompson confirmed her husband's roots as a guitarist: 'He had never worked acoustically, although people think of him as a folk-oriented artist, or whatever, he certainly never was. He started off playing electric guitar. He'd never played acoustic guitar. He's a rock 'n' roll musician, that's all there is to it!' (In an interview with *International Musician* in July 1981, RT cited James Burton as his seminal influence, but Robbie Robertson, Mike Bloomfield, Zal Yanovsky and Thumbs Carlyle(!) got honourable mentions.)

Together, he and Swarbrick proved they were capable of writing songs very much within the traditional idiom, and that they could make traditional music come alive with electric instruments, without Thompson forsaking his rock 'n' roll roots.

7 There's a Hole in the Wall . . .

Fairport went back to America for a second tour in 1970, and on their return, life at the Angel continued in its own wayward fashion. Thompson was interviewed there in August by Roy Shipston from *Disc*, to whom he revealed a keen interest in archery, songwriting and 'becoming the best guitarist in the world'. Of Fairport, he remarked: 'Things will change, and the style will change, but it will be gradual.'

The changes were rung some five months later, when on Sunday 24 January 1971, Thompson announced he was quitting the group. At the time, Fairport were making a comfortable living from gigging. Also, they had astounded the critics who had written them off after Sandy's departure, and Swarbrick and Thompson were writing songs of a calibre which demonstrated that Fairport need not rely on plundering the library at Cecil Sharp House for material.

In an interview for *NME* some months before, Simon had philosophically accepted the departure of Tyger and Sandy, but added: 'Richard represents the group to me more than anyone. If Ritchie had gone, I would have thought, what can I do now?'

Years later Simon told me: 'Richard announced he was leaving because he wanted to do his own writing, and wasn't interested in performing with us. For me it was the worst thing that could have happened . . .'

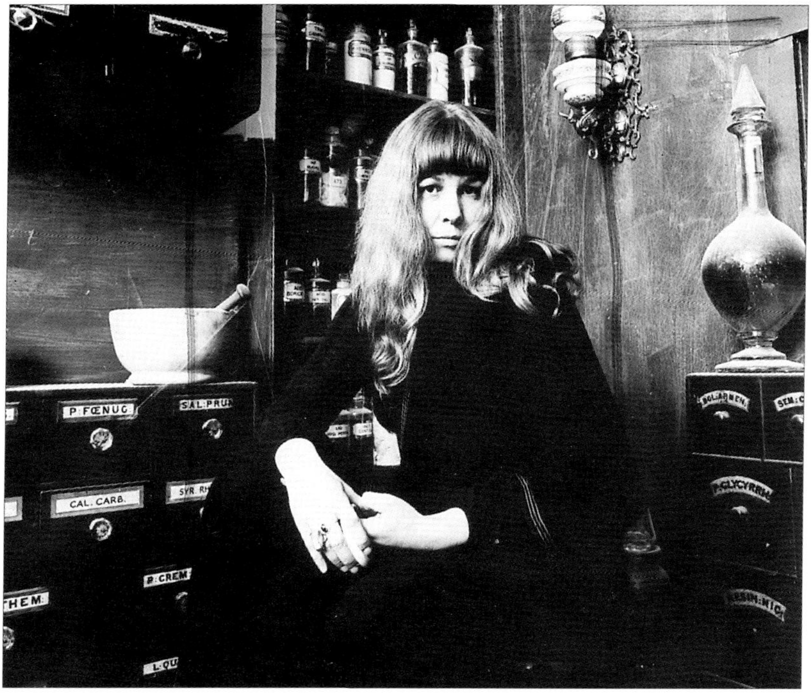
P. FŒNUG
SAL.PRUN
CAL. CARB.
P.CREM
BOL.ARMEN.
P.GLYCYRRH

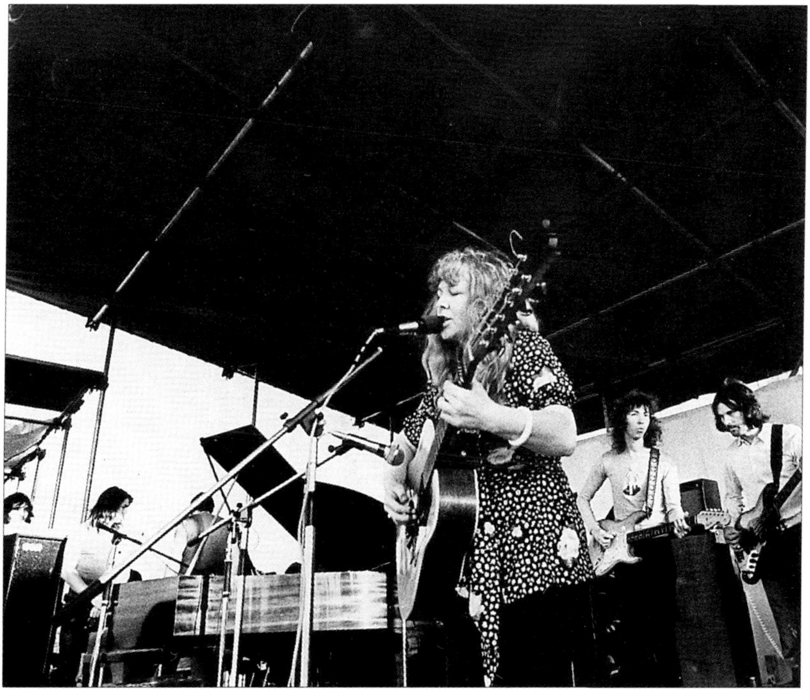

Above: 1884 account of 'The Murder Of A Lady Near Torquay' that inspired Fairport's 1971 *Babbacombe Lee* album
Opposite top: Sandy post-Fairport at the time of *The North Star Grassman And The Ravens*
Previous page below: 1971 Sandy gig, with a little help from Richard and Peggy
Previous page top: Babbacombe Lee tour flyer from 1971 and LP inner sleeve
Opposite below: Stripped of all original members by departure of Simon and DM, Fairport's 1972 all-Brummie line-up. Left to right: Roger Hill, Tom Farnell, Swarbrick, Pegg

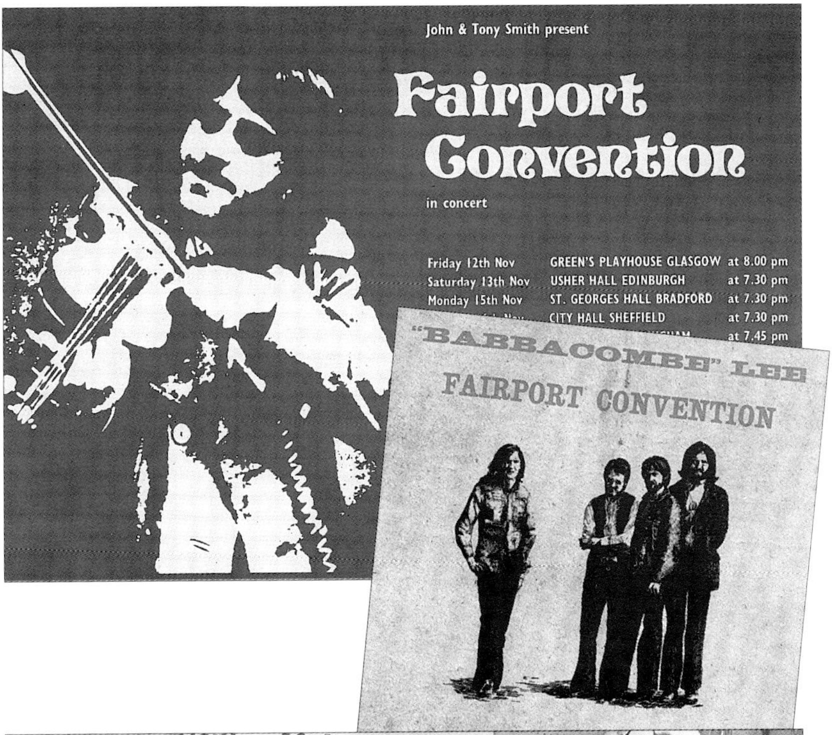
John & Tony Smith present
Fairport Convention
in concert
Friday 12th Nov GREEN'S PLAYHOUSE GLASGOW at 8.00 pm
Saturday 13th Nov USHER HALL EDINBURGH at 7.30 pm
Monday 15th Nov ST. GEORGES HALL BRADFORD at 7.30 pm
CITY HALL SHEFFIELD at 7.30 pm
at 7.45 pm
"BABBACOMBE" LEE
FAIRPORT CONVENTION

Neither Mr Laurel nor

Top: Fairport's tenth line-up, responsible for *Rosie* and *Fairport 9*, introducing Jerry Donahue and Trevor Lucas

Below: Recording at Sound Techniques Studio, 1974. Left to right: Pegg, Mattacks, Lucas, Donahue, Swarbrick

Sandy rejoins Fairport to be with husband Trevor Lucas. Band photographed in St Peter's Square and on the steps of Island Records, 1974

Top: Fairport enjoying life on the road, 1975

Left and below: Richard in the early days of Fairport, and circa 1975, four years after quitting the band

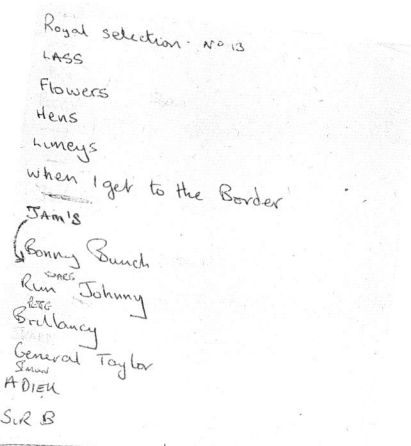

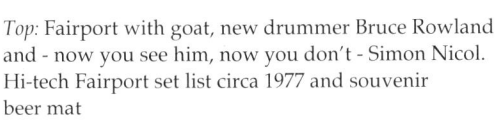

Top: Fairport with goat, new drummer Bruce Rowland and - now you see him, now you don't - Simon Nicol. Hi-tech Fairport set list circa 1977 and souvenir beer mat

Below: Fairport in 1976 pub horror shock drama! Left to right: Dan Ar Bras, Pegg, Swarbrick, Roger Burridge, Bruce Rowland, Bob Brady

Fairport Split 1979. Definitely final-ever performance, last chance to see, never again, etc.

7 There's a Hole in the Wall . . .

Thompson himself was plainly unhappy continuing with Fairport. He was never really fond of touring, and Fairport's two American trips that year had taken their toll on him. When I spoke to him at the end of 1979, he spoke about his reasons for leaving: 'It goes back to what I was saying about *Liege & Lief*; I just felt there was a dimension missing . . . the music just wasn't right. I was writing stuff that wasn't right for the band – the sort of songs which ended up on *Henry* and *Bright Lights*. In a sense it broke my heart, but it was a gut instinct. Fairport's approach was limited . . . I was trying to do English rock 'n' roll, and play traditional music with electric instruments, which I felt could be developed further.'

In a *Sounds* interview in 1972, just before the release of *Bright Lights*, Thompson explained his reasons further: 'I wanted independence . . . Sometimes I think it's very important to think for yourself musically, and at the time with Fairport I didn't do that at all. I was always thinking in terms of the band, and in a lot of ways it was holding my musical ideas back a lot.'

Thompson continued living at the Angel for some months after his 'leaving'. Simon: 'There was no question of a parting of the ways, but he didn't want to go to America again. He wanted to sit in his room and study astrology, just didn't want to go on the road. He wrote songs, tore them up, wrote more songs . . .' (Thompson once described his 'destruction rate' as 'probably nine out of ten'.) Initially, there was some rancour at Thompson's departure. Fairport were preparing for their next album, when at a rehearsal he announced there was no point rehearsing any of the new songs he'd written, as he was leaving anyway! Shy, retiring individual that he may be, Richard Thompson is possessed of a strong, determined character, which balanced perfectly in the Fairport context with Swarb's extrovert nature.

Richard Thompson's contribution to Fairport Convention

was enormous, from his prowess as a guitarist in those early Muswell Hill days, right up until *Full House*, where his talents as a uniquely brilliant songwriter are enshrined. Along with Sandy, he contributed a number of songs to Fairport which helped them establish their distinctive reputation. Throughout his writing career, Thompson's songs have dwelt in the gloomy shadows of a society where success is the accepted standard; a society which has little time for those who fail to achieve that standard. With loving precision, Thompson depicted those 'failures', managing to get under the glossy superficiality and sympathise with those that never really made it. Not for him the heroin hypersensitivity of James Taylor or the emotional spring cleaning of Joni Mitchell. Thompson's songs with Fairport (and beyond) are thoughtfully crafted exercises of depth and feeling.

Tempted by the Lucifer of fame and fortune (Thompson was seriously considered for membership of the Eagles at one time, and Steve Winwood had thought about asking him to join Traffic), Thompson perversely turned his back and set off into the wilderness of the folk clubs, working acoustically with Linda, and as part of a small group with Sandy. He lent his distinctive guitar sound to a number of memorable albums, including Nick Drake's *Bryter Layter*, all of Sandy's solo work, and others by Mike Heron, John Martyn, John Cale and the Watersons.

Finally, in 1972 he released his first solo album, the brilliant *Henry The Human Fly*, which contained some of his best compositions. Even though he was far from happy with his own vocal contributions, the album still stands (I feel) as his finest work.

1974 saw the release of the first Richard and Linda Thompson album, *I Want To See The Bright Lights Tonight*, a stunning combination of Thompson's writing, singing and playing, and Linda's beautiful singing. The album is rich in Thompson classics, and one song – 'The

7 There's a Hole in the Wall . . .

End Of The Rainbow' – is perhaps the *bleakest* song ever to make its way onto record. Richard Thompson follows his Muse to the stark territory where 'Black is the colour and none is the number', where 'Every loving handshake's just another man to beat' and 'There's nothing to grow up for anymore'! Honestly, it makes Leonard Cohen sound like Barry Manilow!

In 1973, the Thompsons embraced the Sufi faith, recording the stark *Pour Down Like Silver* in 1975 before a three-year period of self-imposed silence, broken only by the 1976 anthology *Guitar, Vocal*. This double album covered rare and unreleased material throughout Thompson's career, from 1967 to 1976. Of particular interest to Fairport fans were the inclusion of 'Throwaway Street Puzzle' (the B-side of 'Meet On The Ledge'), and a lovely version of Roger McGuinn's 'Ballad Of Easy Rider' from 1969.

Thompson's post-Fairport career has been frustrating, in terms of his not having been acclaimed as the superb, uncategorisable talent that he is. The Thompsons have never been short of critical accolades, but popular success has eluded them over their five-year career. Even so, Julie Covington achieved a minor hit with 'I Want To See The Bright Lights Tonight', Arlo Guthrie covered 'When I Get To The Border', Any Trouble did a marvellous version of 'Dimming Of The Day' on their second album, and the Pointer Sisters covered 'Don't Let A Thief Steal Into Your Heart' from the Thompsons' *First Light*. (But, as Linda ruefully recalled: 'Typical! The only one of their albums not to go gold! Kiss of death, putting one of our songs on an album.')

Richard Thompson's career continues in its own haphazard manner. Uninterested in the machinations of the music business, embarrassed by the fanaticism his talent attracts, he plunges on in his own idiosyncratic fashion. Thompson is fed up with people telling him he's a genius, so we won't pursue the point. Suffice it to say that without his contributions to Fairport Convention, and his post-Fairport career, popular music would be an emptier place.

Replacements for Thompson were vaguely considered by the remaining members of Fairport: Bert Lloyd (again!), Martin Carthy and David Rea amongst them. The band decided – for better or worse – to plug on as a four piece. Simon: 'We were faced with three options – (1) The band folding. (2) Some superstar musician – who I was sure I wouldn't get on with – coming in. Or (3) Carrying on as a four piece ... I had no choice, *they* had the choice to carry on without me.'

The four-man Fairport started rehearsing at a 'deceased department store' in London, Barker's of Kensington, which later became Biba's. Simon had to literally come up from behind, to take over guitar as a lead instrument in the vacuum caused by Richard's departure. They rehearsed as a four-man band, to honour existing commitments, uncertain as to what the future held. Simon: 'We had no musical direction. It was a question of getting the material we had done with Richard into a four-piece line-up. We had the gigs, and we had to do an album ... I had totally the wrong type of guitar and amps, which were designed to play behind Richard.' So Andy Horvitch, from the old Muswell Hill days, co-writer of a couple of songs on the first album, and now assisting Robin Gee, was dispatched to acquire an AC30 and a Telecaster!

It had been nearly a year since a Fairport album, and Island were pressing the band for some 'product'. The proposed Fairport album – apart from two instrumentals – was to have been composed of songs either wholly, or partly written by Richard Thompson and (or) Dave Swarbrick. On Thompson's departure, only the instrumentals, 'Sickness And Diseases' and 'The Journeyman's Grace' were retained. Swarb: 'You get all this spiel from record companies about singles – so we went in and did nine!'

7 There's a Hole in the Wall . . .

Fairport's idyll at the Angel came to a dramatic end when a lorry crashed into the house early one Sunday morning in February. A Dutch lorry driver, in a hurry to catch the ferry at Harwich, fell asleep while driving his lorry at the top of the hill leading down into the village and went straight into Swarb's bedroom. Richard, whose room was directly above, was in London that weekend, and his possessions (and room) came crashing down onto Swarb's. Simon: 'We got down to Swarb's room, and he was sitting up in bed, just looking at it all, and not one brick was on his bed! And there were a lot of bricks, as you can imagine when one whole wall and a chimney come crashing down.'

The fire brigade and police were round immediately, and the local butcher brought round a chicken and five pounds of sausages. A bottle of poteen was salvaged from Richard's possessions, and demolished by all concerned within about twenty minutes! That night, Fairport played what Simon described as their 'worst gig ever' at the Croydon Greyhound, which was understandable under the circumstances.

Reviews of the band at that time felt, on the whole, that they managed admirably without Thompson, and that the four-piece line-up covered up any deficiencies with their overall professionalism. Fairport were still committed to playing a great many gigs, which they tackled as a four piece, one of the most unusual being a tour of Hungary in May 1971.

They went over on a cultural exchange, representing 'English folk musicians', and played to farmers and Russian soldiers who didn't speak any English. The continuity of their set was somewhat marred by the need for a translator to appear between songs and explain to the baffled audience just what they had been listening to. (The experience was eventually chronicled by Peggy in 'Hungarian Rhapsody', on *Rosie* in 1973.)

Meet On The Ledge

Angel Delight was released in June 1971, and can hardly be considered a vintage Fairport Convention album. It showed them down, but not altogether out. It was their first album without Richard Thompson or Joe Boyd, and the production chores were split between the band and John Wood. The residues of the Swarbrick/Thompson partnership are featured – 'The Journeyman's Grace' and 'Sickness And Diseases'. In a contemporary advertisement, the inscrutable 'Journeyman's Grace' was explained thus: 'Unfortunately, Richard left before he told anyone what these words are about!' 'Sickness And Diseases' was originally recorded as an instrumental; Richard added the words, then left. Fairport planned to record it as a single, and get soul singer Doris Troy in to sing on it, but the plan fell through (although it *was* quoted in full in a book called *The Love Diseases*, which was a history of VD!).

'Bridge Over The River Ash' was something Fairport seemed obligated to include in their live shows for a long time. Essentially a visual gag, as 'The Fairport Ensemble' on violas and violins rose and fell with the beat, it was – inexplicably – included on *Farewell, Farewell*.

'Wizard Of The Worldly Game' was the fruitful result of a shortlived collaboration between Simon and Swarb. Simon actually wrote only the middle verse, but it boded well for the future. The two traditional tracks which open the album, 'Lord Marlborough' and 'Sir William Gower', are rousing renditions of military derring do, but lack Thompson's rich guitar sound. Obviously, the vocal onus fell heavily onto Swarbrick, and his fulsome version of 'The Bonny Black Hare' is eminently suited to his particular style of singing, but the vocal deficiencies which critics predicted would cause the band problems following Sandy's departure were now making themselves apparent. Bert Lloyd's arrangement of the Copper Family's 'Banks Of The Sweet Primroses' was described by Swarb as: 'A

7 There's a Hole in the Wall...

grade "A" English folk song, not to be confused with the other English folk song which starts "As I laid on my bed on a winter's night"!'

The title track is, of course, autobiographical, each member of the band writing a verse about everyone else at the Angel at that time. Robin Gee, by then managing the band, is noted as 'The Mighty Glydd'. 'The hole in the wall where the lorry came in' marked the end of Fairport's stay at the pub.

Angel Delight landed Fairport an appearance on *Top Of The Pops*' short-lived album spot, where Swarb could be seen dashing between a bewildering array of instruments on one number. Fairport had, in fact, appeared on *TOTP* earlier that year, backing Jonathan King – under one of his many pseudonyms – as Sakkarin, who were high in the charts with their version of 'Sugar, Sugar'. Mattacks played bass, Simon was on drums and Peggy was on lead guitar! The album went straight into the *Melody Maker* charts at number 26. Swarb was 'bloody incredulous' when awoken with the news, but wondered realistically 'whether it will get me an extra hour in bed in the morning.'

The traditional songs on *Angel Delight* demonstrated that Fairport were still intent on following the electric folk course, although the treatment afforded to a song like 'Lord Marlborough' lacked the fire and conviction previously demonstrated on, say, 'Matty Groves' only two years before. Simon admitted earlier that the four-man Fairport lacked a musical direction, and *Angel Delight* – however charming an album it is to listen to – is proof of that. Originally conceived as a collection of possible singles, it was cobbled together into an album to pacify their record company, and Fairport fans could well be unsure of just what direction the band would be going in.

With a drastically honed-down line-up, Fairport's only lead singer and instrumentalist was Swarbrick, and the burden fell more heavily on him than ever. With his writing partner departed, he fell back on his extensive knowledge of traditional music to adapt for the Fairport repertoire. A number of people I spoke to stated quite categorically that their interest in Fairport as a band declined with Swarbrick's growing predominance. With Sandy, Ashley and Richard gone, coupled with Swarbrick's extrovert nature, it was natural that he should be seen as the band's front man, but what should be mentioned is that having got 'the bit between his teeth' about pursuing the electric folk direction with Fairport, he was not keen to concede defeat and return, cap in hand, to the folk circuit.

Over the years, particularly through the thorny patches, the very existence of Fairport Convention owed a great deal to the gritty determination of Dave Swarbrick. During those thorny patches, what they actually accomplished musically may be a moot point, but Swarbrick always kept Fairport Convention going until they reached an even keel again.

8 Knights of the Road

In June 1971, *Disc* carried an interview with Swarb and Peggy's old boss Ian Campbell, which is of interest for his opinion regarding Fairport's handling of electric folk: 'I think I am more sympathetic to that kind of music because I know two of the musicians ... They are very musical, and I think that is their saving grace. I don't think there is any danger of electric folk music taking over from traditional – the danger is that it will be used badly.

'Folk music is alive because it has adapted itself to circumstances, but I don't think electric folk is going to have any lasting effect upon it, it's just an interesting side issue ... Their expenses are exorbitant, we travel with all our instruments in a Ford Zephyr. They can't perform in clubs, so they have to concentrate on making records to appeal to a bigger audience. Then they have to water down the music to make it more like pop music, so that it will sell ... But no one can spoil a folk song. They might make a tasteless record of it, but the song itself is indestructible.'

The project which occupied Fairport throughout the summer of 1971 was the collection of songs which ended up as the *Babbacombe Lee* album. Swarb was rummaging through a junk/antique shop in Ware, a village near Little Hadham, when he came upon a yellowing pile of 1907 *Lloyds Weekly News*, telling the story of – and autographed by – John Lee: The Man They Could Not Hang.

John 'Babbacombe' Lee had been charged with the murder of his employer, Emma Keyes (who had been one of Queen Victoria's Ladies-in-Waiting), and sentenced to death. On the day of his execution, however, the trapdoor failed to open, not once, but three times! Lee then served 22 years in prison, and on his release wrote an account of his ordeal for the *Weekly News*, maintaining his innocence throughout.

One explanation for the trapdoor's consistent failure to open was that it was constructed in such a way by prison labour that when the chaplain stood on a certain board, the device would not spring. However true that was, it was certainly the last time a gallows was constructed by convict labour at Portland Prison. But Swarb also heard 'that the hangman was just bad – a ropey hangman, if you'll pardon the expression!'

Swarb bought the papers, with an eye to writing a song about the character, but realised after reading through them that there was sufficient material for an album's worth of songs. Lee had all the makings of a folk hero, and the background against which the murder and trial took place gave a fascinating insight into late Victorian society. Fairport were grateful for a project like *Babbacombe Lee* to occupy them. A unifying topic was just what they needed at that stage.

The bulk of the material was at conception stage before the release of *Angel Delight*, but Island were keen to get a Fairport album on the market, so *Angel Delight* was put out. The majority of *Babbacombe Lee* was written by Swarb, although Simon contributed 'Breakfast In Mayfair', and collaborated with Peggy on 'When I Was 16'. Bert Lloyd's arrangement of the 1860's traditional 'Sailor's Alphabet' was the only non-original on the album. Peggy: 'It was an exercise in conveying the information and sticking music to it. Swarb did most of the work on that, he was full of energy and working 18 hours a day. That's what you need when somebody like Richard goes. All you have to do is sit back when you're in a band with someone like Richard, because you know he's going to come up with the goods, and all you have to do is play them.'

Impressive as *Babbacombe Lee* is, the album contains inherent flaws, which repeated plays fail to obviate. One cannot doubt Swarb's sincerity in tackling the project, but the writing lacks diversity, and the band's instrumental backing has a monotony unlike any other Fairport album. There was also the perennial problem of an alternate vocalist (although Simon's vocal contributions make one wonder why he was so backward in coming forward). I cannot help but agree with Robin Denselow in *The Electric Muse*: 'Just a touch of Richard Thompson, and it could have been the folk world's *Tommy*.' (Or at least given *The Transports* a run for its money.)

For a four-man Fairport, *Babbacombe Lee* was too much to handle. The individual songs do work in the overall context, but the variety the project demanded was not apparent. Simon's 'Breakfast In Mayfair' demonstrated a pleasantly ironic progression in his writing, 'A Sailor's Alphabet' has a nice, boozy feel to it, and 'Hanging Song' rocks along at a fair old rate, but as an album it fails to hang together (only a small pun intended).

The critical response was generally favourable, praising the band's intentions, but not slow to point out the album's deficiencies. The voice of the judge who opens the album is that of Phillip Stirling-Wall, a retired estate agent friend of a friend of Joe Boyd's, who later became Fairport's manager.

Island did a tremendous job on the press kit and sleeve for *Babbacombe Lee* – 'Don't Hang Babbacombe Lee' stickers sprouted all over London before its release. The interest aroused in John Lee's story by Fairport's album was sufficient for the BBC to make a half-hour documentary on Lee, with music re-recorded by Fairport, in 1975. (The Japanese newspaper which accompanied the album credited Mattacks as playing 'Drums and *erectric* piano' – honest!)

Despite poor sales – it was Fairport's worst-selling album on Island – the Swedish government were sufficiently impressed by the album that they used it as a method of teaching Swedish students how to speak English! (Heaven knows what they made of lines like 'V's for the vangs running from the main shaft'!)

During October 1971, Fairport toured America again, supporting Traffic on a rigorous tour – 24 cities in 28 days. It was there that Simon Nicol's dissatisfaction with the band became apparent. Although the brunt of the *Babbacombe Lee* project had been borne by Swarb, Simon had worked long and hard with John Wood producing the album. When the test pressings arrived in San Antonio, Nicol admitted he was at the end of his tether when the band were underwhelmed by his production. Simon: 'I put so much into it, and it was shot down in flames. There seemed to be no longer a meeting of the minds. I saw Chris Blackwell (of Island) that night and asked for my ticket home, but he persuaded me to finish the tour ... There was no real friction. DM was upset, but the other two were fatalistic.'

Fairport toured Britain in November to promote the album, a two-hour show, the first half devoted entirely to *Babbacombe Lee*, the second to older Fairport classics. It was during the second half of their show at the Rainbow in London, that Sandy Denny and Richard Thompson joined them onstage for a medley of old rock 'n' roll numbers, which gave Trevor Lucas the idea for *The Bunch* album that was recorded the next year. Sandy also contributed a spellbinding version of 'The Weight'.

During that November tour, there was 'an incident' at the Van Dike club in Plymouth, when Fairport – described

8 Knights of the Road

in the *Private Eye* report as 'a popular singing group' – were 'entertaining some 450 young people'. About halfway through their set, 170 policemen swarmed into the club, flashing searchlights and keeping snapping Alsatians in tow. Sixteen people appeared in court charged with obstruction, and six others were remanded on bail on suspicion of possessing drugs. None of the Fairport mob were charged.

Simon Nicol was, at that time, Fairport's longest-serving member, the only original from the Muswell Hill days, and the man whose house the band were named after. His last official gig with Fairport Convention was at Dublin's National Stadium on 3 December 1971, but, according to him, 'The following night I did the first reunion gig at Cecil Sharp House.'

His reasons for leaving, as previously mentioned, were involved with the band's reaction to his production of *Babbacombe Lee*, but he had been far from happy with his role in the band after Thompson's departure. His role in Fairport should never be underestimated – although not a prolific writer or guitar virtuoso, Nicol contributed a great deal to the band in rhythmic and emotional stability. Simon: 'I was very happy to be the rhythm guitarist from the first time I heard Richard play . . . I've always thought of myself as a group performer, and what I contributed was for the overall effect'. Many people often spoke of Simon and Richard as perfectly balanced guitarists, like Hank Marvin and Bruce Welch, and were disappointed at his decision to leave, as it severed the final link with the old, 'real' Fairport. Joe Boyd, for one, felt it was 'ridiculous' for the band to carry on as 'Fairport Convention' after Simon left.

Much later, Simon spoke to me of his reasons for leaving: 'Even though it had been a year since Richard left, I was only just beginning to find my feet as a player, and I didn't *enjoy* going on stage in those days. I was exhausted, all the way through that time. I was working at keeping my head above water, in danger of drowning in the music all the time. I had to fight all the time to be a guitar player ... I was trying to play like Richard, to be Richard *and* Simon, I was trying too much. There was a tremendous amount of effort, and *that* was really the reason I left. Listening to tapes of that time, I don't recognise that person playing, it's alien to me.'

Peggy: 'The empathy between Richard and Simon was just totally magic. Simon never had to fill Richard, no one was expecting him to play that kind of guitar, but he was so good at it.'

Simon Nicol's departure marked the end of an era for the band. With no original members left, an uncertain musical future and the disappointing sales of *Babbacombe Lee*, the writing really did look as though it was writ large on the wall for the band who – in the phrase of *Melody Maker*'s Michael Watts – 'had rung enough changes to keep even the most ardent campanologist happy'. Finding Nicol's replacement proved an almost impossible problem for the remaining members, and his departure marked the beginning of the most confusing and non-productive period in the band's already stormy four-year history.

Fairport were in desperate need of someone to exorcise the spirit of Richard Thompson, which still loomed large in any evaluation of the band. While Simon Nicol struggled manfully to fill the lead guitar role, he found the pressures too demanding, and split, leaving a stalwart rhythm section and Swarb. Much as the latter revelled in being the band's focal point, it was patently obvious that Fairport were in need of an equally strong vocalist and alternative lead instrument.

Initially, the guitarist's role was filled by another Birmingham musician, Roger Hill, an old mate of Peggy's from the Ugleys. Hill was in the process of forming a Country Rock band with bass player Rick Price – formerly of the Move, and another Brummie – when he went into Fairport. He was by no means a folkie, although he had worked in Tom Rush's backing band when the American singer had toured Britain. Hill came in on Peggy's recommendation. Swarb was sufficiently convinced that here was the man suited for the guitarist's spot in Fairport, and the three Brummies got on famously during rehearsal. But enigmatic drummer Dave Mattacks was far from happy with the way things were going, or rather weren't, and announced he was leaving on 3 February 1972. Peggy: 'There just wasn't enough in it for him, trying to recreate the atmosphere without Simon.' DM departed, and went into the Albion Country Band straight away with Simon and Ashley. He kept the Fairport connection further intact by playing on the Bunch's album that year.

With Mattacks gone, Fairport were left with an impressive list of European and American dates, and no drummer! A mate of Roger Hill's – Tom Farnell – was roped in at the last minute, just prior to joining the *QE2*, where he was to be part of the ship's band. A standing joke at the time was that the prime condition for joining Fairport Convention was not how well you played – but whether you came from Birmingham.

Farnell's background was that of jazz and big bands, and he joined Fairport with a scant knowledge of folk music. But at least the band had a drummer, and could honour their commitments.

Peggy: 'It was like going on holiday with your three best friends. It was done on that level, and we did the gigs. We never went down badly, but musically it was not good. Not anybody's fault – it wasn't the people you were used to playing with, and it didn't feel like a Fairport band.' The material attempted was fairly unambitious, drawn in the main from *Angel Delight* and *Babbacombe Lee*, and occasional attempts at 'Sloth' and 'Walk Awhile' from *Full House*. That particular line-up scored a lengthy feature in *Rolling Stone* on a short Dutch tour, and played at Amsterdam's 'Folk Fairport' club, which was named after them. Peggy said at the time: 'The bloke I felt sorriest for was the Dutch promoter. It's got to the stage now where he meets the plane and never quite knows who's going to turn up!'

But none of the band felt really confident about getting stuck in a studio and attempting to record an album, which was a wise decision. A tape in circulation of a radio broadcast they did in New York displayed Fairport at their most musically unadventurous, going through the motions, and sounding like a scratch band assembled to fulfil concert obligations.

Fairport Convention Mk 8 called it a day when 50 per cent of the Brum contingent split – Hill on to Chris Barber's jazz band, and Farnell back to the Birmingham beat circuit. That left the two Daves, Swarbrick and Pegg, as sole inheritors of the Fairport mantle, with conspicuous vacancies in the roster.

From across the ocean, Canadian David Rea entered, whom Fairport had already considered as a possibility when Simon originally left. They had worked with him at the Los Angeles Troubadour, and Rea was thoroughly impressed with the band, indicating that if ever a vacancy occurred, he would love to be considered.

In the event, Rea received a call from Fairport when they were touring in Scandinavia asking him to join, and he flew over to join them at the Manor, where they were recording what, eventually, was released as the *Rosie* album.

David Rea grew up in Toronto, and was part of that city's burgeoning folk community, which also included Neil Young and Joni Mitchell. Rea learnt to play guitar, he claimed in a 1972 *Sounds* interview, mainly from the Rev. Gary Davis. He had worked as a guitarist with both Gordon Lightfoot and Ian and Sylvia, and it was while touring with Lightfoot in England that he first met Swarb, who was then still in the Ian Campbell Folk Group. Rea had collaborated with Mountain's guitarist Leslie West in writing three of that 'supergroup's' biggest hits – 'Mississippi Queen', 'Yasgur's Farm' and 'Flowers Of Evil'. His two solo albums had been produced by Mountain's Felix Pappalardi (a man with an extraordinary career, ranging from being Tom Paxton's back-up guitarist to Cream's producer).

Rea arrived while Fairport were struggling to get an album underway, and even by their standards, *Rosie* was a bastard to get finished – in fact *starting* it was proving a seemingly insoluble problem. A brief glance at the sleeve credits indicates the problems: Ralph McTell, Richard and Linda Thompson and Sandy Denny all weighed in with contributions to a Fairport Convention that – during its interminable recording – had virtually ceased to exist. The finished album was only one of three which were considered, but the previous two were ditched in favour of the version that was eventually released in March 1973.

David Rea spent two months working with Fairport at the Manor, and the sessions were, according to Peggy, 'a bit of a disaster'. Rea's inclination was to lead the band in a heavier, rock direction, which neither Swarb nor Peggy was happy with. Tom Farnell was still helping out on drums at those sessions, but nothing serviceable materialised. Peggy: 'It didn't work out. You can never tell on paper what's going to work, it's all a question of people's involvement in it.' It was nothing to do with personalities. Swarb, Peggy and Rea all got along, but working together it became apparent that it was not going to work on record. Peggy: 'It was sad, but everybody knew at the end of the two months, when we played the tapes. We knew it would have to stop.'

Something positive was also needed to stop the rot that was eroding Fairport. It had been some time since an album, and Island were concerned about the disarray apparent in the Fairport camp. Peggy: 'As far as Swarb and I were concerned, it was all over. There was nothing we could do then, there was only really the two of us. We wanted to keep the band going . . . but all the people we wanted to be in it weren't around, or were involved in other projects, and we were getting fairly desperate, because when you work on a project and it all goes wrong, you get pretty low.'

During that period of flux, between *Babbacombe Lee* and *Rosie*, the only Fairport album available was the lovingly compiled, double retrospective, *History Of Fairport Convention*, which was issued in November 1972. While not containing any new material, it acted as qualitative proof of Fairport's achievements throughout their five-year history. The lavish sleeve (incorporating a Pete Frame family tree) benefited from John Wood's lucid and informative sleeve notes.

Even for the avid Fairport fan, it was a useful and instructive package, chronicling the band's metamorphoses. The critics were full of praise for the compilation, but the general feeling around that time was: 'Fine, here's an example of what you have done. What happens *now*?'

The seventh cavalry came in the lanky, Antipodean shape of Trevor Lucas. He was living locally, knew Swarb and Peggy of old, and was keen to help out in producing the album Fairport *had* to get finished.

Trevor Lucas was born in Melbourne on Christmas Day 1943, and became involved with music from an early age. He formed a C&W group and rock 'n' roll band in Australia, before he set his bootheels a-wanderin' towards Europe and became involved in the blooming folk scene there. He finally arrived in England via a circuitous route: Istanbul, Greece, Yugoslavia, Switzerland, Italy and Spain. On the way, Lucas had gained quite a reputation on the folk club circuit with his vivid interpretations of Australian folk songs, and appeared at the Royal Festival

8 Knights of the Road

Hall and the Cambridge Folk Festival. He first came to public attention with the excellent Eclection in 1967. Eclection only recorded one album for Elektra (produced by Ossie Byrne, who was then handling production chores for the Bee Gees). They were a distinctive band, fronted by the stunning Kerilee Male, and one of only two non-American bands to record for that prestigious label, which housed the Doors and Tim Buckley, amongst others (the other non-American act being the Incredible String Band).

Eclection eventually split in October 1969 (their guitarist Georg Hultgren changed his surname to Kajanus, and went on to form Sailor, who enjoyed a number of sizeable hits in Britain during the early seventies).

Lucas was by now emotionally involved with Sandy Denny, and from the remnants of Eclection they extracted drummer Gerry Conway, and together with Pat Donaldson and Jerry Donahue went on to form Fotheringay. Sadly, they only recorded the one album in 1970, Sandy's first venture after she left Fairport. The choice of material on the album was inspired – the haunting, traditional 'Banks Of The Nile', Dylan's 'Too Much Of Nothing', Lucas's 'Ballad Of Ned Kelly', Sandy's 'The Sea' and the joint Denny/Lucas 'Peace In The End', which alone is worth the price of the album.

When Fotheringay eventually split in early 1971, halfway through recording an unfinished second album, Lucas worked as an engineer at Island Studios and was involved as producer on Sandy's albums. He could also be found twiddling the knobs on the rocking 'n' rolling *Bunch* album.

What was left of Fairport were stuck with the Manor tapes, and took them up to Sound Techniques for a reappraisal. It was there that Trevor was involved in post-production work on Sandy's second album, and he, Swarb and Peggy got talking about the possibilities of Trevor coming in as producer to try and salvage something usable from the tapes for the new Fairport album. In a 1973 *Sounds* interview, Trevor spoke of the Fairport which existed during that convoluted period: 'It existed in some sort of weird, spiritual way – but it came really close, I think, to folding as a group.'

Without too much prompting, Trevor Lucas was persuaded to become a full-time member of the band. Three drummers were credited on the sleeve of *Rosie* – Timi Donald helped out on three tracks, but was committed to working with his band Blue; Gerry Conway came from Fotheringay, and also worked on three tracks, but was in great demand as a session drummer, working constantly with Cat Stevens.

So Fairport's manager, Phillip Stirling-Wall, managed to coerce Dave Mattacks back into the band to occupy the drum seat. Mattacks had been working with the Albion Country Band, which was in the process of folding at the same time as Fairport were looking for a drummer. Equally pressing was the band's need for a guitarist. Simon had only just left, and although both Richard Thompson and Ralph McTell helped out on the finished album, obviously neither could join Fairport full time.

Jerry Donahue, after the demise of Fotheringay, was doing session work in London, and Lucas suggested to the other two that he would be an ideal guitarist for Fairport. Peggy: 'I didn't think for a moment that Jerry would join the band ... I had been to his luxi/plush flat in London, and thought, blimey, there's no way he's going to rough it with us.' Fortunately, he was, and he stayed with the band for three and a half years. Donahue was the only American to join this essentially English band, and his stint with Fairport went a long way towards helping them to recapture their former glories.

Donahue was born in New York in September 1946, but spent his early years in Los Angeles. His father Sam had his own big band and worked with Glenn Miller and

Tommy Dorsey. Young Jerry studied piano for four years, but became entranced by the rock 'n' roll sounds coming from the radio, particularly guitarists like Link Wray and Duane Eddy, which made him want to take up guitar.

He came to England in 1961 to continue his education, and also started playing in pubs with bands like the Tumbleweeds and the Cliches. He made one single for Phillips in 1965, 'What's The Matter With Me?', as half of a duo called Dec and Jerry. It was while Donahue was working in Selmers Musical Instruments shop in Charing Cross Road that he met Ray Smith, and went with him into Poet And The One Man Band.

The nucleus of that band went on to form Heads, Hands And Feet, which featured the astonishing Albert Lee on guitar, Tony Colton on vocals (who also produced the second – and best – Yes album, *Time And A Word*) and Chas Hodges on bass, now finding fame as half of Chas and Dave. Donahue did the backing vocal arrangements for the first HH&F album in 1971.

The original guitarist with Fotheringay was Albert Lee, but he only stayed with the band for a fortnight as 'there wasn't enough for me to do'. On his departure, he recommended Donahue to Trevor Lucas as the right guitarist for them. Donahue attributed Fotheringay's short, but memorable, existence to Joe Boyd's insistence on telling Sandy that she should concentrate on her solo career (she had just won the *Melody Maker* award for Best British Female Singer for the second consecutive year) and not jeopardise her future by remaining with Fotheringay. They eventually split, after only one album, although one track – 'Late November' – was salvaged for Sandy's first solo album *North Star Grassman And The Ravens*.

Between leaving Fotheringay and joining Fairport, Donahue worked for a year as part of the backing band to French superstar Johnny Halliday (along with Gerry Conway and Mickey Jones of Foreigner). He also played on Gary Wright's *Extraction* album, and was in the Mick Greenwood Band immediately prior to joining Fairport. On becoming a permanent member, Donahue's guitar jelled perfectly with Swarb's fiddle, and he admitted he felt he really broadened his playing by joining in with Swarb on hitherto unknown traditional tunes.

Finally, after their most unsettled period, Fairport Convention were back together as a band, and moved away from the period which Lucas characterised as: 'Guess the line-up and win a prize!'

The *Rosie* album that was finally released in March 1973 suffered from the fluctuating personnel and dissent which had nagged Fairport during its recording. At last they had a vocalist of distinction with Trevor Lucas, who also contributed a couple of strong songs with his partner Pete Roach, in 'Knights Of The Road' and, particularly, the dignified 'The Plainsman'. Lucas's presence helped endow Fairport with a stronger, richer sound.

The only traditional song was the instrumental 'The Hens March Through The Midden And The Four Poster Bed', which had been recorded during the abortive Manor sessions, and previewed on *The History Of . . .* album. The bulk of the writing credits went to Swarb, who contributed the lovely title track (one of his finest vocal efforts), which displayed a discipline in his writing that his other contributions to the album lacked. 'My Girl' and 'Me With You' are essentially lightweight, non-Fairport songs, but 'Furs And Feathers' recalls the rich Swarbrick/Thompson period, with its driving beat and interesting lyrics.

The traditionally oriented 'Matthew, Mark, Luke and John' has a strong chorus, stirling Donahue solo and *sounds* like Fairport Convention. Although *Rosie* could hardly be considered a classic Fairport album, at least it displayed a *band* at work, and that solidarity boded well for the future.

9 Fiddlestix

Nineteen-seventy-two had been a bad year for Fairport. They had only played some 30 or so gigs, and were in a terrible financial state, but Island gave them £9,000 for a new PA, which boosted their sound *and* confidence. The rhythmic nucleus of Peggy, Swarb and Mattacks was now augmented by the two new recruits and, all things considered, things were beginning to look brighter for the band.

Fairport Mark 10's first gig was in Germany in September 1972, but their biggest was the vast Ngarauwahia Festival in New Zealand in January 1973, where they ended up supporting Black Sabbath! Fairport played their set just as the sun was going down – 'Not a bad light show to have,' recalled Donahue – and were ecstatically received. It was at that same festival that Sandy Denny's solo set included a stunning unaccompanied version of Richard Farina's arrangement of 'Quiet Joys Of Brotherhood', and it was also at that gig, thinks Donahue, that the seeds were planted for Sandy to rejoin Fairport at some future time.

The band undertook a 32-date British tour to promote *Rosie*, and were well received by critics who cared about Fairport Convention. A lengthy world tour followed, with dates in America, Australia, Holland, Denmark and Finland. Sandy Denny joined them on stage in Los Angeles on 9 May, which helped fuel the 'Fotheringport

Confusion'. One of Sandy's reasons for leaving Fairport initially was to be closer to boyfriend Trevor Lucas. Now, with the wheel come full circle, he was back touring extensively with her old band while she laboured with furthering her solo career, and ne'er the twain would meet.

Prior to their next world tour, Fairport started laying down tracks for their crucial next album, proof positive that here was a Fairport with stability as well as musical prowess. Jerry Donahue's instrumental 'Tokyo' (which has been described as a 'Japanese bluegrass number') was the first track they recorded, and which they played a lot on stage when touring. Peggy: 'We did it at this gig somewhere, we knew we were going to put it on the record, and we said to Jerry, "You'll have to get a publishing deal together, make a bit of money out of it." And he said, "Oh gee, I never thought of that, perhaps we shouldn't do it on stage tonight, somebody might rip it off." And I said, "Anybody who can hear *that* once and remember it is welcome to it!" '

Fairport's stage set during those days was a balanced blend of old and new, which showcased the excellence of the two new members, and drew upon all stages of their career. They included two Dylan songs they never recorded, 'Country Pie' and 'George Jackson'. As they were still going out under the moniker 'Fairport Convention', people still expected to hear a generous proportion of their earlier work. But 'Fairport Convention' was an organisation as malleable as putty. With eight albums and ten different line-ups to their name, Fairport Convention could now mean anything from the instrumental complexity and traditional tastes of Swarb and Peggy to the rock 'n' roll predilections of Trevor Lucas, and also manage to incorporate the poignant lyricism of Sandy Denny and Richard Thompson. Fairport Convention – particularly at this stage of their career – had the Damoclesian sword of their (*recent*) past hanging over their present.

9 Fiddlestix

It was something which Trevor Lucas was obviously aware of, as he recalled in that 1973 *Sounds* interview: 'When you get "Meet On The Ledge" shouted at you, you think people really have been away on holiday for five years . . . It's a bit of a disadvantage for us, because people are always shouting out for things like "Walk Awhile" and "Matty Groves" – if you had much sense you'd realise that they're not conceivably possible with the line-up changes . . . I mean it would be ridiculous for us to be doing something like "Angel Delight".'

It's the abiding problem which faces any working rock performer, trying to find a balance between old favourites (which you may well feel stale performing) and new material (which you are proud of, and wish to demonstrate to an audience who prefer older songs). It was a problem which particularly affected a band like Fairport, with so many line-up changes and alumni, and it was also quite an unsettling experience for the die-hard Fairport fan, wondering just who they had paid to see on a particular night.

There had been an 18-month delay between their last two albums, and Fairport were determined to prove their stability by releasing another album as soon as possible. Ironically (considering the circumstances), *Fairport Convention Nine* was their best ever post-Thompson album. Peggy: 'Everybody was really productive in that line-up, it was – more or less – a rebirth . . . It had a lot going for it; socially we got on really well, we were working a lot and did some really good concerts.'

Nine is a consummate Fairport Convention album, acting as a testimonial bridge between the 'old' and 'new' Fairport with its judicious choice of material and performance. It offers Trevor Lucas two lengthy opportunities to demonstrate the resounding timbre of his rich voice. 'Polly On The Shore' is a traditional song, brilliantly reworked by Peggy, which had been included on the Martin Carthy/

Swarb album *Prince Heathen* in 1969. A beautiful song of war and parting from a loved one, it benefits from Lucas's sensitive singing, as he dreams of standing once more 'Alone with me Polly on the shore'. 'Bring 'Em Down' is a lavish working of a traditional theme from Lucas's own pen, a dark, brooding encounter with 'four ghostly riders' (of the Apocalypse?), with a texturally fascinating fiddle exercise from Swarb.

The album also gave Swarb an opportunity to prove just how sensitive a singer he could be, on his adaptation of Richard Lovelace's timeless poem 'To Althea From Prison'. Too often Swarb's vocals lacked subtlety, but 'To Althea . . .' is made all the more effective by his restraint, notably during the famous 'Stone walls do not a prison make . . .' verse.

The brash opening 'Hexhamshire Lass' and the instrumental 'Brilliancy Medley And Cherokee Shuffle' proved on-stage favourites for many years. Donahue's 'Tokyo' was a perfect showcase for his talent. 'Possibly Parsons Green' was a nod in the direction of Bob Dylan's 'Positively Fourth Street', and was also the part of London where Trevor and Sandy shared a flat. It was followed by the strong country-influenced song 'Pleasure And Pain', which was taken at the time for a drug song, but as Swarb explained in a *Melody Maker* interview soon after the album's release: 'What the song is saying is: when you have the blues, when you get really fed up with who you are, don't get angry – that's the reds – because that's going to make it worse. Don't go mixing those reds along with the blues.'

Nine picked up a lot of good reviews from the music press, who welcomed this revived Fairport back with open arms. The general consensus of the critics was that it was a pleasure to be able to review a strong, new Fairport Convention album, that didn't contravene the Trades Description Act! ('Don't Look Now, But The Line-Up's

9 Fiddlestix

Changed', was the ruefully suggested title for *Nine*, by Dave Mattacks. He was also responsible for the enigmatic 'Sorry dear, Rabelais' off' on the back sleeve.)

After an unmatched period of flux, Fairport actually looked as though they were about to achieve the stability crucial for their survival. *Nine* built on all their past triumphs and mistakes, and showed that they had lost none of their traditional flair and were still capable of writing strong new songs. *Fairport Convention Nine* was the album they *had* to make to retain their credibility, and prove their viability.

Peggy recalled that period with great affection: 'It was much more of a group, because everyone was writing from the word "Go" ... We were gigging a lot, so a lot of the stuff had been well played in ... It's one of my favourite records, there was a lot of thought in it. I think that five-man band – had it stuck together – would have gone on to do greater things, because we all got on well and there were never any kind of arguments.

'It was very productive; we should have done another record with that line-up. There had been a couple of years when we didn't gig in London because we'd never had a secure line-up, and no one wanted to go out and play; everything was a bit iffy. But that line-up was gigging five nights a week, and we went back to the colleges again – which were always great for us – because we didn't know whether we could fill the halls, and we couldn't afford to take risks, so we started from scratch ... It *was* good, when you feel confident on stage and you can hear what everyone else was doing, you know it's good. You have Mattacks behind you giving some stick, and Jerry and Swarb, and Trevor singing, it was a great band. Different from any of the other Fairport line-ups, because it approached a lot of different kinds of music. We could do other people's songs with quite a bit of confidence, and we'd got two lead instruments again, which were both very strong, and Swarb didn't have to worry about singing, which he was never happy doing. Of course Trevor loved singing, so Swarb could concentrate on the fiddle, and everybody was doing what they really wanted to do ... But there were all the problems you get with any Fairport line-up!'

Fairport embarked on a massive world tour in January 1974, with Sandy Denny on board in her official capacity as Mrs Trevor Lucas. The air was naturally thick with rumours that she was to rejoin the band, an idea which found favour with a number of members. Jerry: 'Sandy had always been associated with Fairport, and it made perfect sense to me. Obviously Trevor was keen ... But Swarb and Dave Mattacks were the last to come round to the idea, I suppose as they'd been in the band when she left first time around.'

So, eventually, Sandy did return to the fold which many felt she should never have left in the first place. In one sense it was a mistake, as the *Nine* line-up could have capitalised and built upon their own writing and talents, but having Sandy Denny back with Fairport Convention certainly made sense at the time.

Her years between leaving in 1969 and rejoining in 1974 had not been idle. After the premature demise of Fotheringay, Sandy worked on her first solo album, *North Star Grassman And The Ravens*, which featured Richard Thompson, Fotheringay and the Dransfields, and was released in 1971. The album featured only one traditional song, 'Blackwaterside', a customary Dylan cover in 'Down In The Flood' and the surprise inclusion of Brenda Lee's 'Let's Jump The Broomstick' (jumping the broomstick is an old Romany tradition which the bride and bridegroom do three times before a marriage ceremony). Some of Sandy's finest solo writing was also featured, most impressively the majestic 'John The Gun'.

The lavish *Sandy* followed in 1972 – cover photograph

by David Bailey, contributions from Sneaky Pete Kleinow and Allen Toussaint alongside the familiar names of Richard Thompson, Pat Donaldson and Timi Donald. The choice of material for the album was immaculate, containing songs by Richard Farina and Dylan, and Sandy's most accessible compositions. It *should* have been the album which gave her the commercial success which had eluded her. But England, with that curious notion of inverted snobbery, preferred the American efforts of ladies like Linda Ronstadt and Joni Mitchell, conspicuously ignoring Sandy's sterling albums.

Sandy guested on Led Zeppelin's fourth album, dueting with Robert Plant on 'The Battle For Evermore', and contributed to Lou Reizner's overkill version of *Tommy*, for which she received a gold record! She had toured with Richard Thompson and a small band, but immediately prior to rejoining Fairport, she had been touring the States for two months, completely solo, as an opening act for groups like Loggins and Messina, an experience she found daunting.

Her brilliant third solo album, *Like An Old Fashioned Waltz*, was issued in October 1973, and she included the lovely 'Solo' and the evocative title track on stage when she rejoined Fairport the following year. Her prime reason for going back was the fact that she was missing Trevor very, very much indeed.

Japan was the first stop on the tour. It was the first time that Fairport had visited the country, and they went down well. Sandy joined them on stage for a couple of numbers at one show, but they spent most of their time there rehearsing the augmented six-piece line-up for their forthcoming Australian dates. Fairport were the first rock band to play the newly opened Sydney Opera House, on 26 January. The shows were taped, and formed the bulk of the *Fairport Live Convention* album which was released later that year, the remainder being taken from shows at the Rainbow and the Fairfield Halls. The selection of the tracks was decided in the main by Trevor and John Wood.

The band delighted audiences with their effervescence, and the punters were glad to see Sandy back in the ranks, but in financial terms the tour was a disaster. The sheer cost of keeping a band that size on the road was enormous – the air fares for the equipment alone almost bankrupted the band. According to Peggy, the cost of the tour was about five times more than they had actually earnt! Fairport parted company from their manager Phillip Stirling-Wall, and Sandy's brother David took over managing them. Fairport were left owing a vast amount to the travel agents who had transported them round the world. Peggy: 'They must have thought we were some kind of big-time band to run up the bill in the first place, and they never pestered us for six months, God bless 'em.' Island eventually bailed the band out, the cost being written off against future royalties.

It was not the first time Fairport had run into financial difficulties, and it certainly wouldn't be the last. Peggy: 'In situations where we either coughed up thirty thousand quid, or it's the nick for five years, Island have bailed us out. They literally kept us out of the nick, with tipstaffs and bailiffs knocking at the door . . . Most groups get into terrible financial situations, but then most groups don't get into terrible financial situations by *working*! We were esteemed by A&M in America, because they reckon they lost more money on us than any of their other bands!'

In America, Fairport played a number of important shows, including opening for Renaissance at the New York Academy of Music on 17 June. Renaissance were assisted by a 24-piece orchestra, but Fairport had no need for such frills, and stole the show. One of the oddest couplings of that tour was when they supported Weather Report in Kansas. Quite what the earnest jazz aficionados of Mr Zawinul's group made of Fairport is, sadly, not known.

9 Fiddlestix

Fairport Live Convention was issued in July 1974, and is a fairly accurate representation of their live set at that time, covering many facets of their career. As Fairport's first live album, it was an impossible task to fully capture their musical history, or at least spread it over a double album. But as a permanent reminder of Fairport Mark 11, seven years on from Muswell Hill, it is a fine record.

The playing is exemplary throughout, notably Jerry Donahue's bewildering array of guitar pyrotechnics, and Peggy and DM's stirring rhythms. It was an eclectic choice of material: two tracks from Sandy's first solo album (although 'Down In The Flood' had been attempted by an earlier Fairport incarnation); the title track from *Rosie*; a lengthy 'Matty Groves' (with an uneasy vocal from Sandy); a stunning 'Sloth'; and three scorching instrumentals, which display that line-up at its best. A novelty was Sandy and Trevor's version of Chris Kenner's 'Something You Got'. Kenner was a New Orleans gospel singer, who had a local hit with the song in 1963 – he also composed the oft-covered 'Land Of A Thousand Dances'. Lucas was curiously under-represented on the finished album, although live, his vocals were a tremendous asset to the band.

The frantically fast 'Fiddlestix' had been recorded before, around the time of *Nine*, with a 50-piece orchestra! Peggy remembered that particular idea as one of Trevor's experiments. Although it cost a fortune to record, it was only issued as the B-side of a Fairport single in Australia.

Fairport were gradually restoring their reputation, the live album received mainly favourable reviews, and they were doing a lot of gigs, but in between dates there were problems. In a band with such volatile personalities as Sandy and Swarb, confined at close quarters when touring, minor problems became exaggerated. With Sandy and Trevor together, any marital problems were exacerbated by the unreality of life on the road. They were dogged by business problems – Fairport's desire to broaden their appeal globally meant touring, and that in turn meant spending money.

But it was with a confidence gleaned from their touring that Fairport entered Olympic studios at the end of September to start work on their eleventh album, with – at Chris Blackwell's suggestion – Glyn Johns as producer. Johns had worked extensively with Dylan, the Beatles, the Stones and the Who, and had never heard an album by Fairport Convention!

'Rising For The Moon', 'One More Chance', 'White Dress', 'Dawn' and 'Restless' were recorded during that period with Dave Mattacks. Fairport then departed on another American tour and managed to finish the album early in 1975.

Dave Mattacks left (again) in January, clearly dissatisfied with the business problems and managerial instability which threatened the band. Since leaving, Mattacks has enhanced many an otherwise forgettable album with his precise percussive work, including a session for Max Bygraves. Of somewhat more merit was his work with the Albion Band, Gary Brooker, Kate and Anna McGarrigle, and Richard and Linda Thompson. His live work is infrequent, and latterly he has disappeared into the netherworld of sessions. Mattacks' distinctive drumming was an invaluable asset to Fairport Convention, as Simon said of him at the time of *Liege & Lief*: 'He was inventing a whole new style of drumming without knowing it.' On a good night, to see DM and Peggy meshing together, giving the band a solid foundation on which to build, was an inspiring sight.

Fairport were left without a drummer, on the eve of a European tour. Peggy recalled auditioning 30 drummers during 'one of the worst weeks of my life', before they settled at the last minute on Paul Warren, who had been a Fairport roadie for four years. He was a great fan of

Top: Gasp! Fairport back together again, rehearsals at Putney's Half Moon for first Cropredy reunion, 1980

Below: Ticket for second reunion held at Broughton Castle, 1981 - 'Bert Jansom', who he?

Richard Thompson

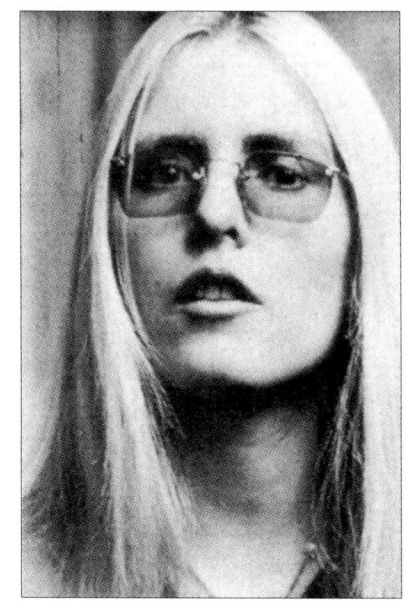

Judy Dyble

Dave Pegg

Ian Matthews

Trevor Lucas

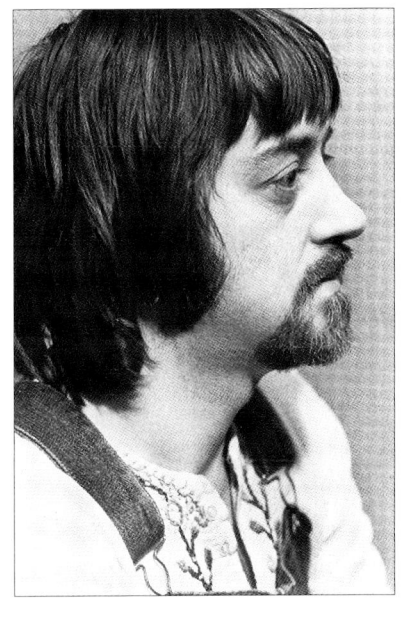

Sandy Denny

Dave Mattacks

Dave Swarbrick

Top: Pegg and Mattacks at first rehearsal for *Gladys' Leap*, 1985

Below: Early days of the most enduring Fairport line-up, backstage at Cropredy 1986. Left to right: Mattacks, Maartin Allcock, Ric Sanders, Pegg, Nicol

Top: Long-time Fairport colleague Ralph McTell, onstage at Cropredy

Below: Aerial view of the festival site

Right: Band with Cynthia Payne, and (with luncheon vouchers) the legendary Johnny 'Jonah' Jones

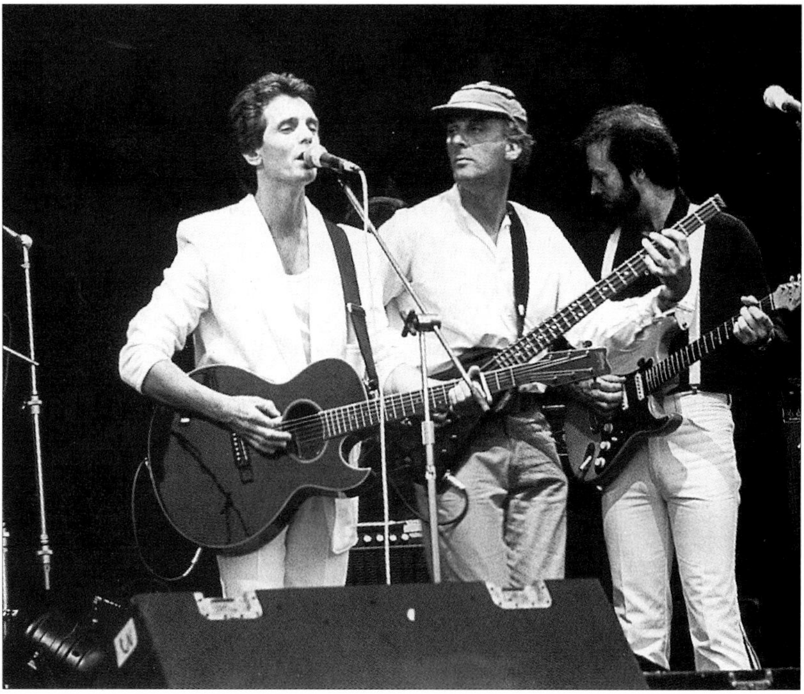

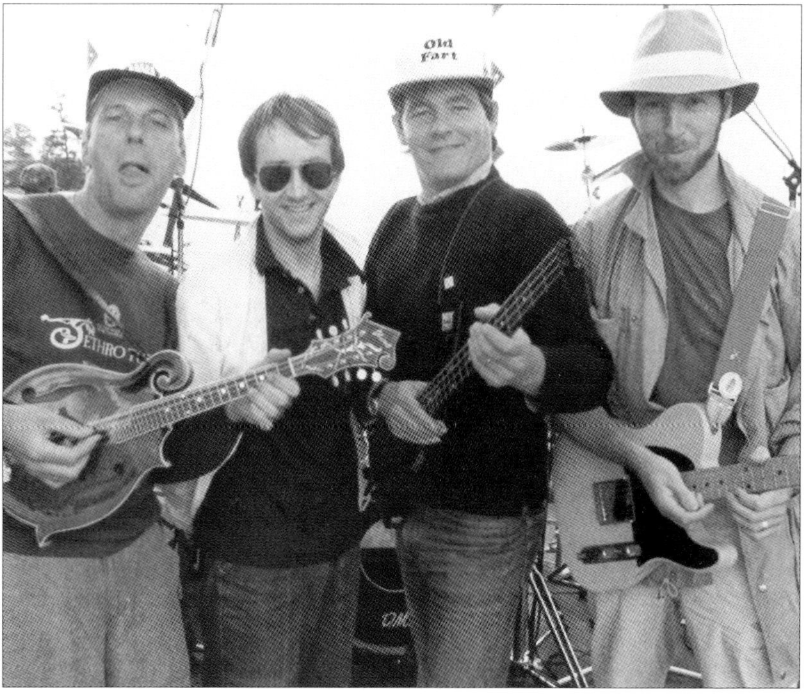
Old Fart

Opposite top: Ian Matthews (left) joins Fairport onstage, Cropredy 1986

Opposite below: All the young dudes? Pegg, Mattacks, Nicol, Thompson together again

Above: Duelling fiddles, Ric Sanders and Swarbrick battle it out at Cropredy

Below: Two men, three guitars and not enough plectrums to go round!

Top: Fairport 1997 on their 30th-anniversary tour

Below: Following the departure of Maartin Allcock, newcomer Chris Leslie completes the current Fairport Convention

DM's, and inevitably his playing reflected that of his hero. Also, he only had to rehearse with the band for a couple of days, as he knew all the relevant material. On completing the tour, Warren went back to roadying, then into a band called Bandit.

Rising For The Moon was, according to Peggy: 'the real miracle Fairport album ... I thought, "This is the end! We've got no finished songs, no drummer, and nobody's talking to each other!" Within a week it was all finished and mixed. Glyn Johns was a genius.'

The band decided that *Moon* was to be a completely different type of Fairport album, which was the reason Glyn Johns was brought in at considerable cost, severing the final link with old Fairport connections by marking the end of the band's fruitful relationship with producer/engineer John Wood. (Wood still worked with ex-Fairport people, though. He engineered Sandy's last album *Rendezvous*, and worked with Richard and Linda, as well as Squeeze, the McGarrigles and Any Trouble.)

As Bob Woffinden noted in *The NME Encyclopedia of Rock*: 'They had a name and a first-rate reputation, but had never achieved anything in America and were not expanding their British audience. They needed another album as fresh and exciting as *Liege & Lief*.' They had the band to do it, too – instrumentally, vocally and lyrically – and the amount of effort Fairport put into *Rising For The Moon* indicated that it was a real make or break effort.

Peggy: 'We rehearsed very hard and got a lot of new songs together, a lot of Sandy's material, because she was the best writer out of all of us. Whether it was the right or wrong thing for the band, you don't think about at the time. You can say, "Right, we'll knock off for a year and we'll make a great record," like Fleetwood Mac. But with Fairport you could never afford to do that, decisions were made fairly quickly, like over a pint in the pub ... We figured, "Right, we've got new material, Sandy's a great singer, and with Trev it will be great because they're both good singers and they're obviously going to be happy working together. We'll have all this material, the record company are pleased, we can get Glyn Johns to produce a record . . ." We did everything we set out to do, and in the process we lost Dave (Mattacks), who didn't like working with Glyn.'

It was Glyn Johns who suggested Bruce Rowland to replace DM. Rowland was born in Park Royal, Middlesex, and first came to the public eye as drummer with Joe Cocker's Grease Band, performing with him at the (in)famous Woodstock Festival. He also made two subsequent albums with the Grease Band after Cocker left, and was the drummer on the original double album of *Jesus Christ Superstar*. A stint with Ronnie Lane's Slim Chance preceded a lengthy spell as a session drummer, before he was coaxed into Fairport and going back on the road. At least with the addition of Rowland, Fairport had a full band to finish the album and undertake gigs to promote it, but the various problems which threatened the group's stability were by no means resolved.

Jerry Donahue too was dissatisfied with the way things were going – while admiring Rowland as a drummer, he felt his style was not right for Fairport. Donahue also felt the finished *Rising For The Moon* album was a compromise: 'We should have gone all out for a new sound. Things like "Iron Lion" and "Let It Go" on one album . . . the sound was of too many people thinking about solo albums.'

Peggy: 'Glyn was putting the pressure on everybody, and Sandy couldn't really cope with that . . . but we had a good crack at it. It was the hardest we ever worked, everybody got stuck in 100 per cent. We all did our best and we thought the record would do quite well, but it didn't, and that was the end of the band!'

9 Fiddlestix

Rising For The Moon was finally released in June 1975, and was obviously a completely different type of Fairport Convention album. For a start, it is the only one of their many albums not to feature the consoling 'Trad. Arr. Fairport' credit. It also has the first of their album sleeves to feature lyrics. It strikes me as three or four solo albums struggling to get out from an album masquerading as a Fairport Convention record. Five of the eleven tracks are solo Sandy efforts, and have a sound strongly reminiscent of her best solo work, but would have sounded better in that context.

The opening (title) track is a forceful beginning, and a promising omen for what is to follow, featuring as it does some of Sandy's deftest, most atmospheric writing. The two Trevor Lucas songs, 'Restless' and 'Iron Lion', are showcases for his strong voice but mark little progression from his writing on *Rosie*, and fail to capitalise on the strengths he demonstrated on 'Bring 'Em Down'. 'Stranger To Himself' is vintage Sandy, displaying some of her most imaginative lyrics. 'White Dress' is a touching song from Swarb, with a lovely vocal performance from Sandy. Jerry Donahue was unhappy with the version of 'Dawn' which was used – he preferred a more acoustic version which had been recorded. Songs like 'After Halloween' and the sweeping 'One More Chance' are Sandy at her best, combining sensitive singing with rich lyrical imagery, but which – in the context of a Fairport album – tend to shift the axis too far in her direction. It is undeniably a strong, well produced, beautifully crafted album, and one which suggested a number of creative avenues the band could have pursued had they stuck together.

The factions in the Fairport camp were growing more divided, particularly as the album on which so many hopes had been pinned was not finding favour with the record buying public.

The critics agreed that *Rising For The Moon* was their

finest achievement since the halcyon days of five years before, but the album only just managed to make the Top 20, and its relative failure was a decisive factor in the ructions which loomed in the band's immediate future. Initially there were still business problems. Sandy's brother David ceased managing them, and Jo Lustig moved in to look after their affairs for six months, which helped get them on a more even keel.

The band toured America for the seventh time, and were well received in the Fairport enclaves on the East Coast, but lost £12,000 in the process. Peggy: 'We never really cracked America, but it wasn't for want of trying! I still believe it isn't a question of selling a million albums and playing 15,000 seaters every night. We'd have been happy to go over there and play the equivalent of Brum Town Hall!'

The financial insecurity, the lack of commercial success which Fairport thought would come their way with *Rising For The Moon* and growing personality clashes were all contributory factors to the impending split. Peggy: 'We owed a lot of money. Nobody had any money, we weren't selling records. It was getting to a dodgy stage in the music business, where people realised that we were never going to be big, and they were being very careful ... It was like a good final attempt, and after that we said, "Right, we're never going to make it, forget record companies, forget all that. All we'll do is whatever *we* want, we'll just play music we like." '

10 Farewell, Farewell

Just before Christmas 1975, the following semi-serious advertisement appeared in the British music press:

'VACANCIES For Name Band. The long-established pop group Fairport Prevention have the following situations vacant (Yes folks, you must be vacant to apply):

AN EVIL LOOKING, SPACED-OUT FIDDLER (No, this is not an advert for a manager). No applicants over 3' 6" need apply. Wages: 26 ounces of duff grass per week.

BASS PLAYER with that twangy adenoid sound, man. Must be able to consume 18 pints of beer per night.

WHIZZ KID LEAD GUITARIST. Must be capable of wheedly-whooping at 140 miles per hour *and* chasing spotlights around the stage at the same time.

SARCASTIC PERCUSSIONIST. Should be able at all times to play cross-rhythms, poly-rhythms, quadruple flam-paradiddles, triple beat dim-flarapiddles and all that flashy stuff what the plebs can't follow. Strictly *no* straight 3/4 please (Only Buddy Rich and Dave Clark need apply).

HUSBAND AND WIFE SINGING DUO. *She* should: Sing like an angel, look like a dream on stage, possess that indefinable charisma, and be able to start

the chorus at least 16 bars before anybody else. *He* should: Croak dem ole familiar folk songs in the 15 cycles per second range, sport; tell a good story, be able to concert tune 43 guitars in 6 weeks and be not less than 7 feet tall in his drainpipe trousers.
FAIRPORT PREVENTION is protected by the Ancient Monuments Act 1956. P.S. Soundchecks our speciality (about once every vernal equinox!)'

In December 1975, Fairport Convention were split straight down the middle by the departures that effectively sealed the band's fate.

Sandy, Trevor and Jerry announced they were leaving. Jerry put his reasons to me very succinctly: 'I left because it was going downhill too fast, too many wrong decisions.' Trevor and Sandy's marital problems were not helped by the rigours of life on the road, which Sandy hated anyway: 'Honestly, you end up like some spaced-out brain on legs.'

Sandy: 'Had *everything* been going smoothly – the finances, the record company – it could have been quite capable of sparking off, like it had in the old days. On the good nights it was great, a really ace band.' In an interview with Karl Dallas, Sandy looked back on that unsettled period: 'Jerry wanted us all to go and live in California, and we did actually toss up the idea for a little while. When he decided to leave, Trevor and I had a discussion about this together – it seemed so endless, recruiting new members into the band and teaching them the old stuff ... To keep having to re-teach these people constantly is a fruitless task. Although it may sound good, it always loses a little bit of something every time, because it needs a bit of enthusiasm from the people who've known it for 10 years ... It may well have been construed as a mistake, my rejoining in the first place. It's no use crying over spilt milk; we had some very enjoyable times and concerts. We really did do some good stuff from time to time, and for those moments alone it was worth it, so there's no cause for regret.'

Jerry had been living in the States following his father's death, and had settled in California with his wife, commuting to England for Fairport rehearsals and gigs, which he found draining. He told me he was genuinely sorry to leave Fairport, as his three-and-a-half-year spell with the band was one of the most creatively enjoyable of his life. He came to Fairport at just the right time, and with his brilliant guitar playing had helped the band re-establish themselves as a potent musical force.

Soon after leaving Fairport, Donahue was rung by Glyn Johns, who asked him to work with Joan Armatrading, which he did for two happily creative years. He also toured with Warren Zevon, and was last heard of working with Gerry Conway – again – in a new band, Thieves, under the lucrative auspices of Mike Chapman.

Poor Sandy died on 21 April 1978, from a cerebral haemorrhage, after falling down a flight of stairs in a friend's house. On leaving Fairport the second time, she and Trevor stayed happily at home, away from the rigours of the road, with Sandy delighting in just being at home and watching the seasons change. Her final album *Rendezvous*, was released in 1977 – a lovely album, with songs from Richard Thompson and Elton John, and some of her own poignant compositions, like 'I'm A Dreamer', and 'One Way Donkey Ride'. After a three-year break in recording, *Rendezvous* had given Sandy the bug to get working again, and there was talk of her doing an album of Inkspots' songs, and moving with Trevor to the States to try recording there. That same year she gave birth to her daughter Georgia. At Sandy's funeral, her favourite psalm 'The Lord Is My Shepherd' was read, and a lone piper played 'The Flowers Of The Forest'. She was 31 years old.

Meet On The Ledge

While not dismissing her work with Fotheringay, or indeed any of her beautiful solo albums, it is her years with Fairport for which she is most fondly remembered: that soaring, seamless voice urging the band on to new heights, giggling between songs or seated dignified at the piano, delivering a devastating solo piece. Linda Thompson, who knew Sandy from the old folk club days, felt that her best songs were never fully appreciated in their solo context: 'Some of the really brilliant songs got lost, because you were listening to song after song that was a wee bit down. But when you take them out of that, and put them in a different setting, people appreciate them for what they are.'

Sandy was probably the finest female singer/songwriter that Britain ever produced, her style ranging effortlessly from folk to jazz, but she never met with the popular acclaim she deserved and her distinctive talents were appreciated by relatively few people. Those lucky few treasure her songs, and treasure her memory still.

She was later commemorated in song by Kate Bush, Paul Metsers and Dave Cousins.

Trevor eventually remarried, and moved back to Australia with Georgia. He did return to Britain, and undertook a few folk club dates with Swarb and Peggy, popping up at a number of gigs on the Fairport 'Farewell' tour in 1979. He also worked in liaison with John Wood at compiling a boxed set of Sandy's best work, with some hitherto unreleased live and studio songs, which is set for release some time in 1982.

Meanwhile, at the beginning of 1976, Fairport were reeling around like a punch-drunk boxer, the banner still being carried by the stalwart Swarb and Peggy, along with drummer Bruce. They were committed to Island for one final album. *Gottle O'Geer* originally started out life as a Swarbrick solo album, but was used by the band as a means of freeing them from their Island contract.

10 Farewell, Farewell

In the back of their minds, both Swarb and Peggy wanted Simon back in Fairport, but he was involved in the Albion Band, and with various production commitments. So, for the time being, Swarb, Peggy and Bruce took off down to Sawmills Studios in Cornwall to make a start on the next Fairport Convention album. Peggy: 'We got the feeling it was going to be the last one ... In the process we realised that we could only get away with one more, so we thought, "Fuck it, it's probably the last thing we'll ever do! We'll have another Fairport line-up, and we'll get a band together and go out, and if it works, all well and good. And if it doesn't – Goodbye!" '

Guitarist Ian Wilson played on two tracks in Cornwall, but the sessions didn't work out to everyone's satisfaction, and they moved back to London. The Fairport ranks were swelled with the inclusion of Breton Dan Ar Bras, Bob Brady and Roger Burridge. Swarb had done some work with Alan Stivell's band earlier in the year, and asked his guitarist Ar Bras into the new Fairport. Swarb had the idea of a six-man Fairport in the back of his mind, which would expand the group's sound with another fiddle and keyboards. Swarb met fiddler Roger Burridge at the Sidmouth Folk Festival in 1969, and had spent a couple of weeks giving the 12-year-old Burridge fiddle lessons. Burridge's father had been a member of the Yetties, and had admired Swarb as a fiddler, so he was familiar with Fairport's past.

Bob Brady, although born in Dublin, had spent his early years in Birmingham and was involved in that city's prolific group scene. On leaving school he had joined the Prospectors, which had featured ex-Black Sabbath vocalist Ozzy Osbourne. Prior to joining Fairport, Brady had been playing with Roy Wood's Wizzard, and it was fellow Brummie Peggy who asked him into Fairport.

The new 'Big Band' Fairport made their English debut at an open-air festival in the inauspicious surroundings of

Meet On The Ledge

Southend United's ground! Peggy: 'We went off to Germany, and by this time, folk music had really taken off because of all the Irish bands, and Fairport had suddenly got a name there. We had only played there twice, years and years ago, and blew it on both occasions.

'We did a festival once in Frankfurt, and we got on stage paralytic. It was total darkness out front, with bonfires burning all around the perimeter. Simon went up to the mike and said, "Good evening. We are Fairport Convention. I see you've got your fires lit. Going to burn a few more tonight, are we?" And that was it. Total silence for the whole hour. So we never figured we were really popular in Germany. But we thought if you're going to get it together, you might as well not do it in London.

'So we went to Germany, and all the gigs were sold out. We were now a rock band, and we couldn't play any of the folk stuff, and of course it was a joke ... We did a lot of Chuck Berry stuff with Bob banging away on the piano and Dan explaining all the songs in his pidgin English. It was good fun, just like starting again, but it didn't work out. There were too many people, too many different styles and approaches to music.'

In a *Melody Maker* interview in 1977, Swarb drew a veil over the proceedings with a resigned: 'It was my fault. It didn't work, that's all.'

Gottle O'Geer was the final Fairport (the 'Convention' had been temporarily dropped) album on Island. Although never in the mega-sales bracket, Fairport's sales on the label had averaged out at about 20,000 per album. *Gottle O'Geer* was a sad and ignominious epitaph for the band on the label on which they had scored their greatest triumphs. Lacking a definite vocalist, the onus again fell on Swarb, who also helped compose the bulk of the material.

The album was an uninspired and lacklustre affair, with only the traditional 'When First Into This Country' gaining anything from the curious electronic backing which Fairport were favouring at that time.

It was *Rosie* all over again, without the saving graces of either Lucas or Donahue, and the sleeve reflects the band's confusion as to who (or what) Fairport actually was. Gallagher and Lyle were mates of Bruce's from his days with Ronnie Lane, and they contributed the underwhelming 'Come And Get It' (wrongly credited on the label as 'Friendship Song'). Martin Carthy was, of course, Swarb's old cohort from their days in the folk clubs and on Fontana, and his appearance on the record marked their first appearance together on vinyl since those pre-*Unhalfbricking* days – it was a shame it could not have been a more meritorious reunion. As it was, the general impression was of all hands rallying to save a sinking ship.

The instrumental 'Frog Up The Pump' is a pleasant enough track, but the majority of the tracks fall into that maudlin, mediocre area which Swarb was unfortunately prone to. The brass arrangement on 'Don't Be Late' was an interesting idea, but like so much of the *Geer* album, one gets the feeling that it was done as an experiment by a band uncertain of their direction, and willing to try anything. One critic called the album 'a sloppy, ill-focused failure'. As so often before, the critics wiped the dust off their Fairport Convention obituaries, and as so often before, they were premature.

Simon Nicol is credited as engineer on the album, and as guitarist on 'Limey's Lament'. The overtures which Swarb and Peggy had been making happened to coincide with Nicol's desire to get back and work with a functioning live and recording band. Since leaving Fairport in 1971, Nicol had not been idle – he had produced albums by Jack the Lad and Richard and Linda Thompson, but found producing no substitute for playing.

Ashley Hutchings had quit Steeleye Span at around the same time as Simon was leaving Fairport, and the two became closely involved in the nascent Albion Country Band, along with Royston Wood, Steve Ashley, Sue Draheim and Dave Mattacks. It was one of Nicol's most cherished ambitions to see the Albions succeed, but they were fraught with the same sort of personnel problems which had dogged Fairport. Steve Ashley, Royston Wood and Sue Draheim were the first casualties; Martin Carthy and John Kirkpatrick were keen to join, but had to wait for six months before they had finished honouring their solo commitments. So as a stopgap, Richard and Linda Thompson (who were, at that time, working acoustically around the folk clubs) agreed to stand in until Carthy and Kirkpatrick were available.

The Albion Country Band did an album with Hutchings, Nicol, Carthy, Kirkpatrick, Draheim and drummer Roger Swallow (from Ian Matthews' Southern Comfort). The excellent *Battle Of The Field* was recorded in 1973, and contained a splendid Richard Thompson clarion call, 'Albion Sunrise': 'The faded flower of England shall rise and bloom again'. Island were not happy with the changing Albion line-up, and when they were presented with the finished tapes of the album, were reluctant to release it, as there was no band to promote it. *Battle Of The Field* was finally released on the cheap Island Help label in 1976.

During the various Albion permutations, they rehearsed rigorously, something Nicol found rather alien after his slapdash years with Fairport: 'It was then I discovered rehearsals. With Fairport we'd only rehearse for a tour, or when the studio time was booked. Even when we were living at the Angel or Farley, we weren't rehearsing to tighten the set up – we were *working* too hard to need to do it, working something like 250 days a year.'

Simon had obviously kept in touch with Fairport during his absence, and had been mightily impressed with the six-piece line-up that had recorded the *Live* album: 'DM and Peggy were terrifying, fingers in the same glove . . .

10 Farewell, Farewell

Peggy, Swarb and DM were natural players; you'd play it once and it was as safe as houses.'

After the lavish production and time-consuming *Rising For The Moon*, and the comings and goings that made *Gottle O'Geer* look like the casting of *Gone With The Wind*, Fairport were keen to get back to some sort of rudimentary basics. Peggy: 'The only things that work for us are things that you do off the top of your head. The things that Fairport were always good at were things that happened naturally, which is why we wanted to get Simon back in the band ... He was a bit sceptical, but he did rejoin, and for the last two or three years it was a very happy line-up. We were just doing very simple, basic things. We were inhibited because of the fact there were only four instruments in the group ... there wasn't a lead singer as such; everybody had to chip in. Simon and Swarb did all the vocals, and it was just like a little folk band really. There was no big thing about it, we would just go out and do gigs and make records.'

Fairport were now managed by Philippa Clare, who did a lot of hustling, and managed to secure them a favourable deal with Phonogram for six albums. Swarb, meanwhile, had signed to Transatlantic as a solo artist and finally, at the end of 1976, he issued his first album. It surprised a lot of people with its strong traditional feel, and demonstrated to the cynics that years of playing electric with Fairport had not blunted the sensitivity of his acoustic playing.

As Fairport prepared to make their debut on Phonogram, things became complicated when Island pulled the seven-year-old *Live At The LA Troubadour* out of mothballs and issued it. Both Swarb and Joe Boyd agree that it was unique in having 'the world's worst record cover'!

Grateful as Fairport fans were to finally have another album from that rich *Full House* period made available, the band were far from pleased with its release at that time. Most critics, however, welcomed it, some even preferring it to the official *Fairport Live Convention* album of three years before. The extant Fairport were ploughing their energies into their next 'proper' album, which was released in February 1977.

The Bonny Bunch Of Roses was one of those albums that Fairport were able to come up with when all the cards were stacked against them. Like the first post-Sandy album, *Full House*, which amazed their critics, or the excellent *Nine* which rose like a Phoenix from the *Rosie* ashes. *The Bonny Bunch* demonstrated a renewed Fairport making the very best of what was available, aware of their limitations, but revelling in their wise choice of material and instrumental empathy.

The *Full House* line-up had attempted to record a version of the marathon title track, but it was never released, although they did perform it on Radio 1, and at the Halifax Pop Festival in 1970. The song has its roots in a Jacobite ballad, and on the 1977 record it is a Swarb tour-de-force, his frequently abrasive vocals tempered on this version. The 12-minute song builds on Peggy's fluid bass lines, and his is a contribution which should never be overlooked in any estimation of Fairport.

As part of the rhythm section, Peggy laid a foundation for a glorious list of players stretching from Richard Thompson to Jerry Donahue, but he was also capable of making the bass a lead instrument – never ostentatiously, but stolidly wrenching rich patterns from the instrument. It is his tribute to the extraordinary Irish author Flann O'Brien that is the opening cut to *The Bonny Bunch*.

'Adieu, Adieu' had also been attempted by Fairport around the time of the first *Rosie* sessions in 1972, and Sandy had tried a version around the time of *Liege & Lief*. Swarb's 'The Last Waltz' is an efficacious number, which has nothing to do with the Band, and even less to do with Engelbert Humperdinck! It's a lovely, lilting, late-night carousel. 'General Taylor' is a rumbustious sea-shanty, also covered by Steeleye in an earlier life. Richard Thompson's 'Poor Ditching Boy' was borrowed from his first solo album, and Fairport emphasised the strong chorus. Ralph McTell's 'Run, Johnny, Run' was salvaged from the composer by Peggy.

The album was latter-day Fairport at their ebullient best – the vocal spotlight split between Swarb and Simon gave them a fuller, more varied sound, and Bruce was developing his own drum style which, while not as rhythmic as Mattacks', was admirably suited to this particular Fairport.

Peggy described their musical direction at this time as simple folk tunes, going back to the *Angel Delight* period. Peggy: 'No one was writing. Swarb, after *Gottle O'Geer* was put out, got such a pasting from the press about his compositions, especially lyrics, that he stopped writing 'em . . . There's a lot of good songs that you can get from the tradition. If the songs that are already there are better than the ones you are capable of writing – then use them! . . . We only rehearsed for three days, I think, which was mainly spent in the pub playing darts . . . It was easy for us to do, because everybody thought in the same kind of way. Simon, Swarb and I could get things like harmonies together so quickly.'

Quite what Fairport achieved in musical terms during their last few years is arguable. Excellent in its own way as *The Bonny Bunch Of Roses* was, it hardly returned Fairport to their Olympian heights. Simon was a welcome addition, his guitar playing improved by his Albion experiences, but the band were well aware of their limitations. For those who saw Fairport live during the last two years of their existence, it was a frequently eerie experience. They were capable of being brilliant – Simon's rendition of 'Flowers Of The Forest' at a Drury Lane concert in May 1977 was spellbinding – but all too frequently, they became a showcase for Swarb's undoubted virtuosity, and threatened to blot out their past in shambling parody. It could still be fun, but it wasn't really Fairport!

Peggy: 'By this time we had all thought, "This is it, we're all old men, we have got old in the process. We are never going to make it, we might as well just play music that we like. Go out and do gigs if we can get them, and if we can make records – great." '

1978 saw them gigging prolifically, and recording in February at Chipping Norton studios for what would become the *Tipplers Tales* album, released in May. It was, in a way, Fairport's most 'traditional' album, containing such folk standards as 'John Barleycorn' and 'Reynard The Fox' (which they had also tried recording with Sandy).

The album's only outside contribution came from singer/songwriter Allan Taylor, who contributed the breezy 'Lady Of Pleasure'. The lengthy 'Jack O'Rion' gave Swarb ample opportunity to re-tell the tale of 'the finest fiddler in the land'. 'John Barleycorn' had been covered by everyone from Traffic to the Young Tradition, and Fairport's recording was a faithful, driving version of the song.

What proved to be their last album of original material was a disappointment after the eclecticism and experimentation of *The Bonny Bunch*, but it showed a compact, utilitarian band, aware of its limitations. Comparisons are odious, and while Fairport on the whole managed to entertain, and not end up with mud all over its face, it would be unrealistic and untrue to say that the Fairport Convention of *Tipplers Tales* could be favourably compared to, say, *Unhalfbricking*.

As musical innovators, Fairport Convention played a sizeable part in shaping the direction of contemporary English rock music. The richness and breadth of their

10 Farewell, Farewell

material made them unique. While best remembered for *Liege & Lief* and the instigation of the English folk-rock movement, no other band but Fairport could have made albums like *Unhalfbricking, Full House, Nine* or *The Bonny Bunch Of Roses*. Richard Thompson could never have made an album like *I Want To See The Bright Lights Tonight*, Ashley Hutchings could never have rung the changes in the Albion Band, and Sandy Denny could never have written a song like 'John The Gun' without the Fairport Experience.

But while Steeleye Span tore round the world and collected gold albums for their efforts, Fairport muddled along in their own haphazard way, conspicuously failing to capitalise on any commercial prospects, perversely ploughing on, partially out of principle, but mainly due to an inability to seize the time.

I believe that not finding a replacement for Richard Thompson when he left in 1971 was their crucial error. To have tried to replace Sandy after *Liege & Lief* would have been an impossible task, and one which they wisely avoided. But the strengths of that *Full House* line-up were apparent, and when Thompson left, they resolutely gritted their teeth, and contracted instead of expanded. It took them a further three years after that to achieve a line-up which could stand on its musical merits, rather than trade off the Fairport name.

Perhaps Sandy joining a second time was a mistake, but at the time it *did* seem like a good idea. *Rising For The Moon* demonstrated a band with a breadth of experience and talent, and if that line-up had persevered, the writing would have shifted away from Sandy and developed into a more collaborative venture, which would have expanded the possibilities for the band.

But, well, that's Fairport! Part of their appeal lay in their frustrating erraticism. Just after you'd torn up your ticket stub, vowing never, *ever* to see them again, they'd

Meet On The Ledge

come up with an album or a show that really made you sit up, and bear with them until the next time. Those who cared, persevered through those frustrating nights where their cluttered irresponsibility made you give up all hope.

Then there were the great nights, when you saw a band of awesome potential, stretching every which way, and carrying you along on the exultation of it all. Which is why, in its own ramshackle, flawed and frustrating way, *Farewell, Farewell* is as fine a Fairport testimonial as you could wish for.

On that last tour, Fairport were certainly musically better than the performances enshrined here suggest, and the choice of material is curiously random, to say the least. The inclusion of 'The Bridge Over The River Ash' is redundant, and 'Mr Lacey' has no value other than that of pure nostalgia. But there is something sincere and moving in hearing Simon bring it all round again with the anthemic 'Meet On The Ledge'. And it's the drowning man syndrome: just hearing the mnemonic strains ringing through the air, you remember Sandy and Martin, and everything that happened to them, and you, in the 12 years in between.

The album was only intended as a memento of the gigs, and as such 3,000 copies were pressed and sold from Peggy's home, until Simon's Records took it up and ran off 20,000. That, along with their version of Mike Waterson's 'Rubber Band', were Fairport Convention's last *official* records.

Swarb's worsening hearing problem was the ostensible reason for knocking it on the head in the summer of 1979. But for many the writing had been on the wall long before. Peggy: 'I think everybody wanted to break ... I could have gone on forever, just doing gigs, like the Spinners. You might as well play with your mates. If you want to carry on playing, you might as well do it with somebody you like, and everybody was too old and set in their ways to try something new.'

10 Farewell, Farewell

Peggy felt that given, as they say, 'sufficient airplay', 'Rubber Band' could well have been Fairport's 'Day Trip To Bangor', and given the band the shot in the arm it needed to finish on a high note.

The band still owed Phonogram four albums, but the label was less than enthusiastic about the prospect of Fairport staying on after the disappointing sales of *The Bonny Bunch* and *Tipplers Tales*, so the label paid them *not* to make any more records. Peggy: 'Phonogram said, "Please don't make any more albums." And we said, "Sorry, we're going to send you another four, one a month if necessary." In the end they paid us not to make any more . . . but then that's their business. It's the first time we ever made any money!'

Fairport's 36-date, official 'Farewell' tour ran from May through to August 1979, climaxing at Knebworth on 4 August before a devout Led Zeppelin audience. (Zeppelin, as stated earlier, were old mates of Fairport, and specifically asked for them on the bill.) Later that same night they finished officially in front of a home crowd at Cropredy. This tiny Oxfordshire village was where Peggy, Simon and Swarb had all lived at one time or another, and they felt a great affinity for the place. It had been the site of an important battle during the English Civil War in 1644, and the band's local, 'The Brasenose', is pictured on the sleeve of *Nine*. It was a moving and emotional event for all who went along.

But, true to form, the last proper Fairport gig was actually the day after, in Belgium – their 'Raid Over Belgium Tour'. Peggy: 'In all honesty, we were hard up, and when we did that tour we did as much work as we could because we didn't want the band to fold up owing people money . . . All of a sudden, when it was all coming to an end, you discover there were places we could have gone and worked. Like in Italy, there was only us on – and 7,000 people turned up!'

Meet On The Ledge

On the official dissolution, Peggy went virtually straight into Jethro Tull, and finally found the financial security he had lacked throughout his Fairport daze. Swarb went back to the folk clubs, working acoustically, but latterly has been doing fewer and fewer gigs, and spends most of his time on his farm in Scotland. Simon went back to the Albion Band, and working on live dates with Richard and Linda. Bruce has been working with Ronnie Lane again, and keeping his hand in with numerous sessions. They all seem happy, and Peggy feels their reunion gigs at Cropredy could well become a permanent fixture for them all. But, for convenience sake, we shall draw to a close at Cropredy, on the night of 4 August 1979.

It was all over. With a family tree that looks like a Romanov claim to the Czar's roubles, 22 members, 17 albums, thousands of gigs and a 12-year history, Fairport Convention eventually decided to call it a day. They gave a great deal over the years. They were a band of mystery and imagination, of booze and rock 'n' roll, of sombre purpose and knockabout good times. The best and worst is on record, but perhaps the albums simply act as reminders of the gigs. Memory is a strange, selective thing – over the years it tends to exclude the bad things and retains only the best. Which is why, when thinking of Fairport Convention, one tends not to remember the occasions when Swarb was too pissed to play, or when the PA was picking up more extraneous signals than Heathrow, or a lacklustre Fairport line-up was simply going through the motions.

No, what one remembers are the classics, like Richard Thompson tearing off a solo that made the hairs on the back of your neck go on strike, or the rhythmic fluency of Peggy, as immobile as a statue on stage, or Sandy, or Ian, or Ashley or ... so many memories.

11 Country Pie

As was so frequently proved during their erratic history, Fairport never learnt to say 'goodbye'. As already shown, they played a gig the day after their official 'Farewell' gig in 1979. Within a year, they were back together again for *another* show at Cropredy, which also featured Richard and Linda Thompson. This had a lot to do with the fact that Dave Pegg – who slotted neatly into Jethro Tull soon after Fairport's demise – was nothing short of a workaholic. With Tull committed to little more than one album and a tour a year, Peggy found himself with time on his hands. And after all, 'Farewell' is only a word!

The 1980 Reunion was such a success that it was decided to keep it as a regular, yearly event. While other bands split, then come back with all manner of hyperbole concerning 'musical drive' and 'rekindled interests', Fairport quite rightly accepted the limitations of their audience. They obviously still had a lot of fans – not enough to sustain them for twelve months' work a year, but enough for everyone to have a good time once a year.

Also hanging over the idea of any permanent Fairport reunion was the problem of Swarb's hearing. Whatever one felt about Swarb's influence on the band during their later years, there was no denying that a Fairport without Swarb could hardly be called Fairport. In an interview with *MM*'s Karl Dallas in August 1981, Swarb himself admitted that Fairport should have knocked it on the head a good six years before they officially did. He said he felt that Fairport's output during those last years was down to three or four good tracks an album: 'The rest are dross . . . I think *Angel Delight* is good. I think *Babbacombe Lee* stinks now . . .' Interesting, considering that many – both inside and outside Fairport – saw him as the band's unifying constant.

Little oddities surfaced with every gig, like Richard Thompson's 'biography' for the 1981 programme. (Wally Swinburn, the Czab and the Swing-Airs, eh Richard?) Of particular interest to fans was a cassette compiled by Dave Mattacks called *The Airing Cupboard Tapes*. The cassette was culled from various stages of Fairport's career, the earliest being 'Walk Awhile' and 'Sloth' from 1971, actually recorded at Simon's 'last' gig with the band in Texas. Inevitably, the quality was erratic, but there are some sterling Sandy vocals on 'Who Knows Where The Time Goes' from 1974, and 'That'll Be The Day' from 1972. Mattacks also contributed some pungently idiosyncratic notes with the cassette. (Only 137,422 performances of 'Sloth'?)

Peggy managed to get the 1981 Reunion plugged *everywhere*. Readers of the prestigious 'William Hickey' column in the *Daily Express* were informed, as were BBC viewers. Fairport were also filmed by Granada TV for a special, which included an imaginative arrangement of 'Now Be Thankful' with the CWS (Manchester) Silver Band, who featured prominently on the Thompsons' first two albums. Unfortunately, Fairport overran and the song had to be dropped.

The 1981 reunion took place at Broughton Castle, a few miles from Cropredy. The setting was perfect – a 600-year-old manor house set in the rolling Oxfordshire hills. Nearly 8,000 people turned out over a sunny August weekend to witness all manner of Fairport incarnations.

There was a buoyant feeling in the crowd, perhaps not unconnected with England's victory in the Test Match... and the bottomless tanker of Theakston's beer!

It all really began the week before, at the Half Moon in Putney: for three nights, various Fairport Mafiosi assembled and conducted live rehearsals in public. There, in the back room of a pub nestling near the Thames, I saw them on a clammy August night, which also happened to be my 29th birthday. What better present than the *Full House* line-up in blistering form? The great thing about that gig was that it wasn't simply an excuse for nostalgia. It displayed five great musicians at the peak of their form, nurtured by experience, strengthened by their five years apart. Balanced, fulfilled, and trusting each other, Fairport conjured up music which obviously evoked the past, but which refused to rely on it. Seeing them play that night was an enriching experience, and one which fully confirmed their stature as a great band.

Obviously the nature of 'reunion' gigs is nostalgic, but from the very moment Swarb, Simon, Peggy and Bruce took the stage in the early evening, it was obvious they were not content to rest on their laurels. DM joined them for an intricate rendering of 'Angel Delight', and throughout they played with a fire and vigour many bands would envy. They injected their set – drawn mainly from *Bonny Bunch* and *Tipplers Tales*, as well as old favourites like 'Brilliancy Medley' – with a passion they had lacked during their last years as Fairport.

The dusk had settled by the time Richard Thompson made an appearance, to a cheer rivalled only by the announcement of Ian Botham's 118. Thompson is a notoriously shy individual, eschewing the accolades which periodically float his way, but that summer he seemed to have found the buzz for playing live again, and infused that enthusiasm into his playing. His *Strict Tempo* instrumental album had been well received, and despite the problems associated with his and Linda's Gerry Rafferty-produced album, he was obviously getting off on playing with his old Fairport colleagues. He had played some scorching guitar with the GPs earlier in the week (a scratch band with Ralph McTell, Peggy and DM, working their way through old Hank Williams, Jerry Lee Lewis and Richard Thompson numbers, which Karl Dallas called 'the most exciting musical experience of your life!').

Throughout that magical week, Thompson's playing was honed to a pitch, as if he'd saved all his best work for the occasion. He threw himself into his playing with an intensity which left the audience gasping, and the heights he attained obviously sparked the others off. I'd never heard Simon, for example, in better voice – his handling of 'Matty Groves' was masterly, juggling around with phrasing, and singing with an intensity which was remarkable. Balancing off against Richard, Swarb mustered some of his best playing in years, helped, no doubt, by the success of his best ever solo album, *Smiddyburn*, which reunited the *Full House* mob with John Wood. Whereas the later Fairport had tended to become over-reliant on Swarb's pyrotechnics, with Thompson in tandem, his fiddling was spellbinding.

An unexpected detour down Memory Lane came with the appearance of Judy Dyble. As willowy as ever, she dashed onstage with the *Full House* mob, nervously sang her way through 'Both Sides Now' and 'When Will I Be Loved', before scampering off into anonymity. The band charged through a comprehensive set, including 'Poor Will And The Jolly Hangman', 'Now Be Thankful' and a majestic, 20-minute version of 'Sloth'. Peggy contributed a mesmerising solo, and so intense was Thompson's playing that he broke a string during *his* solo! The song became imbued with a life of its own, like watching a slumbering giant flex his muscles. It fully vindicated Fairport's decision to re-form, and made me proud to have been there to hear it.

11 Country Pie

Fairport were joined by Ralph McTell at the end of the night, who delivered an emotive 'White Dress' in memory of Sandy, before *les toutes ensembles* poured their all into a stirring 'Meet On The Ledge'. It was one of those moving musical evenings, hearing a favourite band on the peak of their form, singing for their friends on a balmy summer night. And that song, so tied up with their illustrious past, but still a song full of hope for the future. As everyone there sang along with the band, we all had our own memories of them, of ourselves, of friends, of what had been and what was to come. It was a long way from a church hall in Golders Green, but a lot of people who cared about the band were there, singing along. We found a sense of purpose, and formed an emotional bond with that band, that night. If you *really* mean it, it all comes round again . . .

12 Postscript

It seems somehow eminently fitting that I should be writing this while listening to a tape of the new Richard and Linda Thompson album *Shoot Out The Lights*. Without doubt, it's their most consistent album since *Bright Lights*, a suitably high note on which to end this book which, at times, threatened to give Tolstoy a run for his money!

In re-reading the finished manuscript, I notice all its transparent faults. It's too strong on quotes, but that seemed the best way of telling Fairport's convoluted story. A number of people felt that it read too much like a long feature, and if I had my time all over again, I'd probably try and inject more of *me* into it, not purely out of ego gratification, but simply to try and get more of a flow going. I wrote it as a Fairport fan, and still feel it's the sort of book I'd want to read in that capacity.

Enough apologies. The last chapter finishes with the triumphant Fairport Reunion of 1981. By now the album of the show will be available, proof positive of just how good it was. There's a lot of songs Fairport never officially released now available. Judy Dyble's version of 'Both Sides Now', Dylan's 'Country Pie', Jerry Lee Lewis's 'High School Confidential' (shame that there's no GPs album!) and Richard's own excursion into 'Lola' territory on 'Woman Or A Man'.

Richard has gone from strength to strength. *Strict*

12 Postscript

Tempo established him as England's premier guitarist, and *Shoot Out The Lights* consolidated his success. The original version of the album was produced by Gerry Rafferty, and to his credit he was willing to record Richard and Linda with his own money. But it was too lavish, Richard was less than happy with it, and scrapped it. The available version sees him reunited with producer Joe Boyd. Any Trouble's Clive Gregson (a Thompson fan of long standing) contributes backing vocals, and his contribution marks a wheel coming full circle, as Any Trouble had included a sensitive rendering of Thompson's 'Dimming Of The Day' on their fine second album, *Wheels In Motion*. Richard himself contributed the odd session – literally, in the case of David Thomas's (of Pere Ubu) *Sound Of The Sand* album on Rough Trade. He was also called upon to help inaugurate London's prestigious Barbican Arts Centre in November 1981.

The end of 1981 saw him make his first performing visit to America since his trip with Sandy in 1973. He played solo sets in San Francisco and New York, which were ecstatically received. The *New York Times* called him: 'Almost certainly the greatest English composer of contemporary folk music.' Linda Ronstadt, Al Stewart, Mark Knopfler, Loudon Wainwright, Brian Eno and Terre Roche were only some of the celebrities that turned out to see him.

Modest as ever, the last time I saw Richard (thank *you* Joni Mitchell!) in February 1982 he was confident that he had enough material to play two solo sets without repetition! He's his own harshest critic, but now he seems to be achieving the simplicity in his writing and playing that he's striven for, and he's still learning, and broadening his musical horizons. Richard will never rest on his well-deserved laurels. The fact that he can say he is still learning about music is as good a cue for optimism as any I've heard in recent years.

Simon and Swarb are happily out working the folk clubs. Swarb's *Smiddyburn*, which reunited him with the Fairport of *Full House* and producer John Wood, was rightly acclaimed as his best ever solo work. His hearing can stand up to a yearly get-together with an electric Fairport, but otherwise he and Simon are fully booked around the clubs.

Simon is also a full-time member of the new Albion Band. Ashley, as ever, was out to ring the changes. With the bulk of the old Albions tiring of their tenure at the National Theatre, they (John Tams, Bill Caddick, Graeme Taylor, Michael Gregory, Howard Evans and Roger Williams) went off to form the excellent Home Service, with their innovative brass section. They're a grand band, who should by now have resolved their management problems.

Ashley furrowed his brow, and went off to rural isolation to plot his next move. The new Albions began gigging at the beginning of 1982, and were full of surprises. I think a lot of people thought they'd persevere with electric reworkings of traditional songs, but Ashley and melodeonist Dave Whetstone buckled down to serious, contemporary writing, and delivered some marvellous material. Ashley co-wrote the epic 'Wolfe' and the haunting 'Always Chasing Rainbows'. For many people, it was a real revelation, considering the song he was most associated with was 'Mr Lacey' in 1968! The last time I spoke to him, he was justifiably delighted with the Albions. He still felt there was room for development in the folk field, but doubted if *he* was the one to do it: 'I think it badly needed an injection of new blood, of enthusiasm . . .

'We've tackled folk music from a knowledgeable, caring, academic standpoint. Maybe now it's time to tackle folk music without any preconceived ideas or knowledge, to play it as garage music!' Whatever happens, Ashley can now justifiably add 'songwriter' to his list of achievements. As ever, his future moves will be fascinating.

12 Postscript

Peggy is now an integral member of Jethro Tull. He's happy there, gets on well with Ian Anderson, is playing as well as ever and contributing the odd song. Tull only occupy about a third of the year, which allows him plenty of time to organise the various Fairport activities. He and his wife Chris keep busy with their Woodworm Studios, and without their efforts the Fairport Reunions would never have got off the ground. Chug-a-lug!

Dave Mattacks was the only extant Fairporter who wanted nothing to do with this book. Apparently he felt Fairport was only a part of his playing past, and he didn't want to dwell on it. Eventually though, he reconciled himself to the idea, and made a number of constructive criticisms of the finished manuscript. DM's been keeping as busy as ever with session work, and there was even talk of him joining Wings. As it happens, he simply drummed on Paul McCartney's new album, gaining quite a tan from working at George Martin's Compass Point Studios in the Bahamas. He recently worked with Jimmy Page on the soundtrack of the otherwise disastrous *Death Wish II*, and wishes people wouldn't spell his surname Mattocks!

Joe Boyd now has his own label, Hannibal, which numbers Richard and Linda Thompson among its acts. Boyd also went into film production with the 2-Tone film *Dance Craze*, before resuming record production.

Trevor's back in Australia, working as a radio producer. He and Jerry Donahue are the special guests at the 1982 Fairport Reunion. He has produced an album by the Bushwackers, which Peggy described as 'a sort of Australian *Morris On*!' and also contributed a number of unissued Sandy songs to a compilation Island were planning to release in late 1981. I was asked to do the sleeve notes for the three-album anthology, which was planned along the lines of the fine Nick Drake *Fruit Tree* boxed set. But Island got cold feet, or whatever, and the release has been indefinitely set back. In all modesty, I hope this book makes them think again. I tried to persuade them to acquire the rights to material of Sandy's which has never been officially available (like the versions of 'Sir Patrick Spens' and 'Suzanne' which she did with Fairport, which the BBC apparently own), and it would also have been nice to have included unreleased live versions of songs irrevocably associated with her. Anyway, the songs from Trevor's tapes were 'When Will I Be Loved?', 'By The Time It Goes Dark', 'King And Queen Of England', 'Full Moon', 'Moments' and 'Still Waters'. Let us hope they will be available one day.

And that, I think, is that. A long and writhing journey from a North London suburb. Rather than get maudlin by looking back, look to the future: the Home Service and the Albion Band are carrying the torch that Fairport lit.

An essential ingredient of popular music is its ability to change. At the moment it's lightweight, superficial and stylish, but it *has* to have roots. Fairport imaginatively built on those roots, and they deserve at least one book about them. I hope this is the one.

Patrick Humphries
March 1982

Epilogue, March 1997

Meet On The Ledge is the story of a band as they forged their unique path through a particularly turbulent period of British rock 'n' roll. Words like 'seminal' and 'innovative' are bandied around far too freely today, but in the case of Fairport Convention during that incredibly fertile period which encompassed *What We Did On Our Holidays*, *Unhalfbricking* and, especially, *Liege & Lief*, it would be negligent not to use them.

Fairport genuinely did pioneer a completely new sound. Back then it was called 'folk-rock', now it's known as 'English rock 'n' roll', 'roots music', 'Unplugged' ... Whatever you call it, it's forever Fairport.

Long-time Fairport fans can now revel in the material which has surfaced since this book was first published. *Heyday*, an album collecting together the band's classic BBC Radio 1 sessions from 1968/69, was made available on CD in 1987. While Ashley Hutchings' revealing collections *The Guv'nor, Volumes 1–4* provide a fascinating fly-on-the-wall account of the Fairport founder's musical development – 'Washington At Valley Forge' from Volume 1 for example, is historically priceless, as the only Fairport-related track actually recorded at the Fairport house.

Island Records' long-awaited Sandy Denny box set *Who Knows Where The Time Goes* finally appeared in 1985, a fine testament to Sandy's standing; and it was nice to see Sandy's long-deleted 1968 album with The Strawbs made widely available again by Joe Boyd's Hannibal label. Island also recognised the long-running interest in Sandy by including the hard-to-get 'Man Of Iron' on the 1995 *Folk Routes* compilation.

Original Fairport manager John Penhallow, who relocated to Australia in 1975, put together some intriguing collections, *The Attic Tracks*, which brought together rare Sandy and Trevor Lucas tracks. Proceeds from these went to the couple's daughter Georgia, who was orphaned on Trevor's death from a heart attack in 1989. On into the 90s, it is to be hoped that Sandy begins to be appreciated by the same audience who have kept alive the music of the late Nick Drake.

In Fairport mythology, Sandy Denny is venerated. For many, Sandy's haunting handling of the marathon, traditional ballads, embody the very best of Fairport Convention. Each Cropredy sees Sandy's vocal chores handled by various flexible female guests – June Tabor, Cathy LeSurf, ex-All About Eve diva Julianne Regan and Vikki Clayton are only some who have sung under her mantle. Such is Sandy's standing, that when a Sandy Denny tribute band fronted by Vikki Clayton appeared at Cropredy '95, they were called 'The Nerve' (as in 'what a nerve').

Kingsley Abbott, who with his schoolfriend Martin Lamble, was in the audience for the first-ever Fairport gig, rang to tell me that the date of the auspicious occasion was in fact Saturday 27 May, 1967. I had it down as 1 June, the day *Sgt Pepper* was released; everyone else I asked had it down as 1 June, but Kingsley had kept his ticket stub!

The first free concert in Hyde Park was held on 24 August, 1968 – that's free, as in not paying any admission, which is where it differed from the 'Pay To View' 1996 one, featuring Bob Dylan and The Who. The 1968 line-up ran: Ten Years After, Peter Green's Fleetwood Mac, Family, Roy Harper, Eclection and – opening the batting because they had to scuttle off to a gig at Market Harborough that night – Fairport Convention.

Re-reading *Meet On The Ledge*, I'm conscious that I seriously undervalued the impact of The Band on *Liege & Lief*, probably because the Englishness of the Fairport album seemed so fresh and important at the time. But for Richard Thompson, *Music From Big Pink* was 'the album', and The Band's lifestyle and musical integrity were also real influences on the seminal British folk-rock album being carved out at Farley Chamberlayne.

Just when you thought there could be nothing left in the vaults, wonderful things surfaced. Fairport's tranquil reading of Richard Farina's 'Quiet Joys Of Brotherhood' from 1969 was one of the highlights of the Sandy box. While for many, the marathon, Swarbrick-less version of 'A Sailor's Life' which graced 1993's three-CD Richard Thompson collection *Watching The Dark*, was nothing short of breath-taking, showcasing – as if it needed any further showcasing – the fluency and fluidity of Richard's playing.

While always fighting shy of endless retrospective packages, Richard has made a point of occasionally dipping into his bulging back catalogue to dust down the odd Fairport favourite – for example on tour in 1994, 'Now Be Thankful' made a surprise, and welcome, appearance in the set list.

The GPs' album *Saturday Rolling Around*, featuring Richard Thompson, Ralph McTell, Dave Pegg and Dave Mattacks, finally made it, a decade late, in 1991. A rambunctious rock 'n' roll evening, which brought back fond memories of the quartet's 1981 Broughton Castle appearance.

The widespread introduction of compact discs in 1983 helped bands like Fairport Convention and their fans. As well as prompting the re-release of all those old albums, CDs had room for about twice as much music as black vinyl, long-playing records. Bands like Fairport with extensive back catalogues were able to explore the possibility of virtually redesigning their back catalogue on its CD release.

Island, the label with which Fairport are most closely linked, has taken some time to reactivate their albums and fans were a little disappointed when the label's *25th Anniversary Pack* consisted simply of the *Babbacombe Lee*, *Rosie*, *Nine* and *Rising For The Moon* albums transferred straight from vinyl to CD, with neither bonus tracks nor even a celebratory essay.

However, Joe Boyd's Hannibal label, which issues many of his former Witchseason acts – including Fairport, Nick Drake, Sandy and Fotheringay – has added a little lustre to the Fairport back catalogue. As well as *Heyday*, the Sandy box set and Richard Thompson releases, in 1986 Hannibal also released *House Full*, an alternative live souvenir of Fairport's 1970 stint at the LA Troubadour.

Most memories of Fairport's debut American dates in 1970 with the *Full House* line-up are 'a bit hazy', but I for one can't help wishing I'd been a fly on the wall during the drinking contest between Dave Pegg, John Bonham and Janis Joplin at Jim Morrison's local bar in LA.

Fairport also benefited from the appearance of *Q* magazine in 1986, which rescued bands of the Fairport vintage from the hands of inkies like the *NME* – where they were automatically dismissed as boring old farts – and gave them a platform for chronicling their musical history.

Q's first major Fairport retrospective appeared in March 1989. In September 1992, *Q* commemorated the band's 25th anniversary with a piece by Rob Beattie (who went on to write a track on Fairport's 1995 album *Jewel In The Crown*). It was a wide-ranging retrospective, with past and present Fairporters remembering Sandy (Richard: 'the best girl singer in Britain'); abject failure (Peggy: 'some manager comes along and sends you on a world tour which loses £30,000'); and successes (Ashley: 'as the years have gone by the list of people influenced by Fairport has grown').

The most challenging inheritors of the Fairport mantle appeared in the early 1980s: growing out of various Albion Band incarnations put together on the South Bank for a number of different National Theatre productions, arose The Home Service. Masterminded by John Tams – with a brass section as radical in its potential as Fairport's electric guitar peregrinations of 12 years before – The Home Service only stayed together long enough to record two proper albums, but those lucky enough to see them live will long cherish the impact and the memories.

As the man responsible for The Albion Band, Steeleye Span, and The Home Service, it seemed reasonable in 1981 to ask Ashley Hutchings, who after all had also founded Fairport: 'Whither folk and folk-rock?' I still find his answer intriguing, if only for its timing. He replied: 'We've tackled folk music from a knowledgeable, caring, academic standpoint. Maybe now it's time to tackle folk music without any preconceived ideas or knowledge, to play it as garage music!'

Within months of our conversation, the pages of the *Melody Maker* and *Folk Roots* were bursting with news of the new 'Rogue Folk' movement. With hindsight, for 'rogue' (Edward II, Skiff Skats, English Country Blues Band) we can read 'Pogue'. The Pogues lurched onto the scene around 1984, upsetting as many people as they delighted. Richard Thompson hated their stage Irishness; Dave Mattacks loathed 'the punk thing . . . a real celebration of ineptitude'; but for all that, The Pogues were the first roots band of the 1980s to cite traditional music as being as influential on their music as The Clash.

Meet On The Ledge

If The Pogues were the somewhat delinquent new figurehead on the good ship folk, also on board were Billy Bragg, The Bluebells, The Men They Couldn't Hang, The Oyster Band, The Boot-Hill Foot-Tappers, Moving Hearts ... all raising their glasses in the general direction of Fairport Convention. Even as late as 1996, Ocean Colour Scene, tipped as one of the brightest British bands of the 90s, were citing *What We Did On Our Holidays* as one of their favourite albums of the year.

Ashley himself went on through various incarnations of The Albion Band, spent an evening as Cecil Sharp and was also responsible for one of the most sheerly enjoyable ex-Fairport adventures: the 1995 *Twangin'n'A-Traddin'* album. ('So have you ever wondered what a musical meeting of British folk-rockers and musicians specialising in late 50s/early 60s rock instrumentals would sound like?') At the time of writing, the beetle-browed Ashley was busy putting together something special for Cropredy '97. Thirty years on, the alchemist never sleeps.

It is Richard who has enjoyed the most illustrious post-Fairport career. Though mainstream success still may elude him ('Richard who?' is still a common response when his name is mentioned), he has carved a career as a guitarist and, particularly, as a songwriter of real distinction. While the Richard Thompson song catalogue isn't yet as widely covered as Burt Bacharach's, the fact that American acts such as Nanci Griffith, Emmylou Harris, K. T. Oslin and Patty Loveless are recording Richard Thompson originals, can only bring his name to a wider audience.

If Richard's recent career has somewhat eclipsed that of Fairport (1997 Grammy nominee, object of three tribute albums, to date), his affection for the time he spent with the band remains evident. Talking to him at length during the long, hot summer of 1995, for what became *Strange Affair*, Richard became strangely animated when recalling

Epilogue, March 1997

the band's transition from an American-influenced covers band. ('I remember being angry and saying to Ashley, this isn't good enough,' he told me, banging his fist on the table for added emphasis, 'we've *got* to get some original material.')

When I spoke to Clive Gregson about Richard's relationship with his former band, Clive laughed: 'Richard left Fairport in 1971, and he's been playing with them ever since.'

The history of Fairport Convention from the mid-80s on, is the history of the Cropredy Festival. The success of Cropredy is due to the efforts of the indefatigable Chris Pegg who organises the whole thing, from backstage laminates to loo paper. All her husband has to do is stay sober enough to get up on stage and play bass for four hours.

Cropredy has developed into the nicest outdoor festival, with the best toilets, in the UK. Though it is hard now to reconcile the crowds of 20,000, the high-tech stage and the double lines of security fencing with the bumbling, village-bobby Cropredy of not that many years ago, the first sight that greets the hung-over on Sunday morning is still the village's boy scouts assiduously picking up the litter.

While some of the musical choices may seem a bit wayward, and occasionally the Fairport set needs a little editing ('Sloth' is in danger of turning into a mini-series), the music is only one part of Cropredy's appeal. If it is about anything, Cropredy is not simply about Fairport Convention, it is about a community, which happens to have Fairport as its vital link.

As soon as you arrive in Cropredy village on the second weekend in August and see all the Fairport T-shirts, and the crowds milling along the country lanes, tankards dangling from their belts; when you hear the soundcheck drifting over the slowly filling field, as the sun shines down, and you can smell the grass and the breakfasts sizzling ... it could only be Cropredy.

Writing in *Mojo* in October 1996, Andy Soutter was captivated: 'Cropredy and the Fairports seem to stand for something quite important: that deeply ingrained Middle English sense of one nation, of tolerance and compassion; and they're justifiably proud of it, along with that other virtue of self-sufficiency: "We don't rely on the music business or fashion," says Dave Pegg, "we survive from our own devices and it's a very honest way of making a living and we're very happy doing it." Long may they do so. I'll be coming round again.'

Cropredy has grown from 750 people standing in the rain in a former Labour Cabinet Minister's widow's garden, to the 18,000 plus punters it now draws. Fairport themselves are as much an integral part of the event offstage as they are onstage, whether it's Simon Nicol standing chatting by the bar, or Ric Sanders bobbing and weaving around the site. After the music has wound down, the Sunday afternoon cricket match, Fairport v Cropredy, is a sight to behold: Danny Thompson towering over the opposition, Richard Thompson eyeing the hostile clouds, determined to take stroke before the rain. Best of all at the 1996 match was Dave Pegg, manifestly out, but after such a successful weekend, no one had the heart to dismiss him.

Ultimately though, what draws people to Cropredy year after year in such numbers, is Fairport's Saturday night set, now only fractionally shorter than Coppola's *Godfather* trilogy. The band use the Saturday night slot as a platform for a canter through their 30-year career. Though by its nature a backward-looking event, Fairport are still more than capable of playing stirring and uplifting music, music which easily transcends mere cosy nostalgia.

And then there are the guests, the ex-Fairports who break cover from time to time, like Judy Dyble or Ashley

Epilogue, March 1997

Hutchings, Ian Matthews or Jerry Donahue over from America, Trevor Lucas (before his sad death) or Richard Thompson. All happy to rekindle memories of other places and other times.

Memorable 'Special Guests' have included Linda Thompson, Billy Connolly, Ian Anderson, Everything But The Girl, Steve Harley and Procol Harum whose moonlit 'A Salty Dog' was an all-time Cropredy high. In 1986 Robert Plant, making the first of his three Cropredy appearances, was memorable for other reasons. Here was a Rock God made mortal. This was long before Led Zeppelin were officially canonised; the mighty Zep had split six years before, and all Plant's appearances since had been low-key. Seeing the old lemon-squeezer on fine fettle, balancing Zeppelin favourites with forays into traditional territory, was a night to remember.

Another Cropredy delight for me, came in 1995, when Roy Wood ran through a selection of his classic hits from The Move and Wizzard days. The highlight just had to be the bagpipe-friendly mid-August reading of 'I Wish It Could Be Christmas Everyday'.

Much of Cropredy's appeal has to do with the Wadworth's bar, situated at stage right. In excess of 50,000 pints of the Wiltshire brewery's fearsome 6X brew are shifted over the Fairport weekend. More beer is said to be sold at each Fairport reunion than at the Campaign for Real Ale's festival!

But it isn't just falling over that gets you into the Cropredy mood; the stalls which circle the festival site are a nice reminder of happier, simpler times. Delicious vegetarian food, incense and craft stalls, tie-dyed T-shirts and everything Fairport-related you can imagine – even, should you need them, Fairport 'scanty panties'.

Equally compulsive are the souvenir programmes. Year after year, the Peggs still manage to come up with something different for us to read. Thrill here to Dave

Swarbrick's Ideal Alternative Occupation ('Joe Boyd's bank manager'); gasp at Dave Mattacks' Most Memorable Gig ('The Geoff Reynolds Band's opening Saturday night in the Locarno Ballroom, Sauchiehall Street, Glasgow ...'); double-take at Simon Nicol's First Musical Memory ('Sir Patrick Spens') ... Then there are favourite Fairport recipes (Japanese Country Style Bonita Fish gets Richard Thompson's mouth watering), and the opportunity to marvel at the perceptiveness of Dave Pegg's 1963 School Report for Music: 'He has queer ideas on composition and must learn to write according to the rules before he tries to be original!'

Cropredy goes from strength to strength. The crowds increase, the sun always shines (*not in 1996 it didn't! Ed.*) and it shows no sign of ending. As long as extant members of Fairport Convention can totter on to the stage, wrap their arthritic fingers around the opening chords of 'Matty Groves' and last out the epic four-hour set, there will always be a Cropredy. And even if the day comes when they can't, it'll likely keep going anyhow.

Just when you thought you would never live to see them, once again the newspaper headlines screamed: 'Fairport To Split Horror Shock Sensation!' After 11 years, the man christened 'Multi-Instrumentalist Maartin Allcock' was quitting Fairport.

For over a decade, Maartin and Ric Sanders had helped keep the band on something approaching an even keel. As newcomers both had brought a degree of stability and certainty to Fairport; and in tandem with Messrs Mattacks, Nicol and Pegg, Allcock and Sanders had put the brand name back into the band. Though in an institution as venerable and venerated as Fairport, it was inevitable that both Maart and Ric were still regarded as the 'new boys', even after more than a decade in harness!

The long, snaking path which led to the rebirth of

Epilogue, March 1997

Fairport Convention had begun improbably with a 65-year-old Cotswold post-mistress. Gladys Hillier ensured that the mail always got through to the village of Cranham, even if it meant her having to jump over a brook because the plank was always getting swept away. Such dedication to duty was rewarded by the spot being marked on the official Ordnance Survey Map as 'Gladys' Leap'.

This story, reported in the *Guardian*, made Dave Pegg smile. The name had the sort of cosy, middle-England resonance of a Fairport album title. It was an album that Fairport needed to make.

Following their 'official split' in 1979, Fairport had soldiered on in a half-hearted way, meandering together as the occasion demanded. Mostly, the band spent their time going through a door clearly marked 'The Motions'. They reconvened at Cropredy every summer, and if there was sufficient wonga on the table, the quartet could be persuaded to high-tail it off to Europe for a lightning raid on a pop festival.

There were those who felt that Fairport Convention were leaving themselves open to prosecution under the Trades Description Act. They were in danger of becoming what DM always dreaded they would: 'The Freddie And The Dreamers of the folk-rock world'. Desperate measures were required.

Following the '79 Fairport split, Dave Pegg had dovetailed neatly into Jethro Tull; Dave Mattacks had disappeared into the lucrative world of session drumming (Hi Paul McCartney! Yo Elton John!); while Simon Nicol stayed with The Albion Band and performed with Dave Swarbrick as a duo around the folk clubs and festivals.

A few years later, Simon and Peggy found themselves at a loose end, and DM had time on his hands, so the trio got together for a knock. Swarbrick had moved up to Scotland so, familiar with Ric Sanders' playing from The

Albion Band, the three part-time Fairports asked Ric in to play on three tracks for what was shaping up to be *Gladys' Leap*.

When the finished album was released in 1985, it was far better than it had any right to be, banishing the memory of those lacklustre late 70s offerings. The new Fairport reconnected with the 'old' on the opening track, Richard Thompson's breezy 'How Many Times', while making their own mark with 'The Hiring Fair' and 'Wat Tyler', two lengthy folk ballads co-written with their long-time compadre, Ralph McTell.

Swarbrick hated the finished album ('only because he wasn't on it,' said Simon) and refused to play any of it at that year's Cropredy. The situation was becoming untenable: *Gladys' Leap* had got the best reviews of any Fairport album in a decade, the fans' response to the new material was immensely gratifying, and Simon, DM and Peggy were champing at the bit to play it live.

The hearing problems which had dogged Swarbrick for years made it unfeasible for him to front an electric band, and Ric Sanders was raring to go. But in order to replicate the studio sound of Fairport '85 onstage, more even than Ric Sanders was required, and then Peggy remembered a chap who used to babysit for the Peggs ... Just as Live Aid was winding down in the small hours of 14 July, 1985, Maartin Allcock received an enquiry from a Mr David Pegg as to whether he would be interested in joining Fairport Convention.

Such was the success of *Gladys' Leap*, and the subsequent 40-date UK tour which showcased the new boys Allcock and Sanders, that by early 1987, it would not be presumptuous to say that Fairport Convention were back.

When you have been around as long as Fairport, the anniversaries come along with all the hammering regularity of tax demands. Appropriately, to commemorate Island Records' 25th anniversary and Fairport's own

Epilogue, March 1997

20th, the *In Real Time* album appeared on the label still inextricably linked to the band. Besides a lovely anniversary version of 'Meet On The Ledge', the album showed just how well Ralph McTell's 'The Hiring Fair' had slotted into the set, and how timeless 'Crazy Man Michael' really was. Despite the baffling credit for 'Live Sound In Concert' and a cover shot unmistakably taken in front of a Cropredy audience, *In Real Time* was actually a studio album, allegedly with applause from a John Martyn concert grafted on! ('It was something to do with Fairport supporting Tull, and deadlines,' deadpanned Peggy.)

Fairport's 1987 *Expletive Delighted* album showcased the band's instrumental virtuosity. The Fairport palette was enriched by the musical colours Allcock and Sanders had brought along with them, and 'Hanks For The Memory' paid homage to the red Fender Strat which had so inspired an entire generation of Marvin disciples. Reborn and revitalised, Fairport were now once again firing on all cylinders. The infusion of new blood meant that Cropredy was no longer simply a place for fans to go and wallow in 20-year-old set lists; instead, the festival became an opportunity to appreciate new and dynamic pieces as they slotted seamlessly into the Fairport canon.

The next full Fairport album, *Red & Gold* in 1988, confirmed them as a band with a future, as well as a past. Now safely distanced from being a mere nostalgia act, links with the past were still acknowledged by the album's final track, Bob Dylan's 'Open The Door, Richard', which Fairport used to play way back in the 1960s. Ralph McTell again contributed a major ballad, in this case the title track; Dave Pegg adapted traditional singer Archie Fisher's 'Dark Eyed Molly'; while songwriters Huw Williams and Dave Whetstone were familiar names in Cropredy circles.

Reviewing *Red & Gold* in *Q*, Rob Beattie ended: 'This

is the first complete instrumental and vocal set from the "new" Fairport and for a band that's so obviously in it for the crack – everyone gets to do their turn – they still take their music very seriously. The stability's there again, and the next album will be the one to watch for.'

With the release of *The Five Seasons* in 1990, Fairport Convention again found themselves in the record books, with this, the longest serving line-up in their 23-year history. Perhaps the most encouraging sign of this Fairport renaissance has been the increasing confidence of Simon Nicol, not as a frontman – Simon was always a grand stand-up – but as a singer.

In the early Fairport incarnations, Simon was for too long in the shadows – either of Sandy as a singer, or Richard as a guitarist. Now, with the spotlight solely on him following Swarbrick's departure, Simon shone. His singing took on a depth and maturity which were ideally suited to the sort of gutsy material Fairport were tackling.

The Five Seasons was a worthy addition to Fairport's catalogue, if only for Simon's heartfelt reading of the traditional 'Claudy Banks'. Peter Blegvad's 'Gold' and Dave Whetstone's 'Rhythm Of The Time' were too cumbersome to be the major ballads Fairport intended, but 'The Card Song' is a jolly call-in, with Fairport name-checking old friends. Simon handled Huw Williams' 'Ginnie' with sensitivity, and if 'The Wounded Whale' was more *Free Willy* than *Moby Dick*, it was still a noble stab.

Half a decade together, the 'new boys' were playing like old-timers. Ric Sanders' flamboyant violin pyrotechnics contrasted with Swarbrick's solidity, and provided a new dimension. With Maartin Allcock on board, the term 'multi-instrumentalist' for once described a player who added shade and texture to the songs, rather than simply showing off. And as ever, the rock-solid rhythm section of Peggy and Mattacks never missed a beat. The bass and drums men were there, steady and reliable, just as they

Epilogue, March 1997

had been since *Full House* – give or take a few DM detours.

Commitments to Jethro Tull (which at one time boasted Allcock as well as Pegg in its line-up), Cropredy every summer, and the yearly winter tour, all contributed to a four-year delay between Fairport studio albums. But the event which caused the band most concern occurred in 1992, when Ric Sanders stumbled through a plate-glass window in Chipping Norton, severing tendons in his wrist. His place at Cropredy '92 was taken by a young Whippersnapper called Chris Leslie. Fortunately, Ric made a complete recovery, and fiddles ever onwards.

Cropredy '92 was officially Fairport's 25th Anniversary, and a 1993 double CD (cunningly entitled *Fairport Convention 25th Anniversary Concert*) featured guest appearances from Robert Plant, Julianne Regan, Ralph McTell as well as ex-Fairporters Dave Swarbrick, Richard Thompson, Ashley Hutchings and Bruce Rowland.

With the slew of anniversaries in their wake, Fairport knew that to retain their cred, a strong new studio album was now needed. The band's problem, of course, was the absence of an in-house, world-class songwriter. In this Fairport were shadowed by their past; they had, after all, been the first showcase for the talents of a man who many believe to be England's premier songwriter – Richard Thompson.

It was also within Fairport that Sandy Denny had first been allowed to develop her writing, but for all their instrumental brilliance, neither Ric Sanders nor Maartin Allcock felt capable of tackling proper 'songs'. Simon Nicol had long fought shy of the challenge, and while Dave Pegg's 'Hungarian Rhapsody' showed promise, one is forced to concur with the composer, who in 1996 modestly admitted: 'We have no plans to write any lyrics ourselves, because our lyrics are shithouse!'

In concert, Fairport could, and did, happily cover songs

associated with Richard and Sandy, but on record, they needed new material to keep at bay the revivalist image. A Fairport song needs to have a strong narrative, an epic sweep allowing plenty of scope for instrumental soloing, and if it's not asking too much, a memorable chorus.

There was a real danger that if they continued to settle for tackling familiar songs by other writers, Fairport would soon be perceived as little more than a covers band. They needed quality songs which would lend themselves to becoming identifiably 'Fairport'. In the past, Fairport had gone in and knocked out an album in the gaps between tours and Peggy's Jethro Tull commitments, but for their first studio album since 1990's *The Five Seasons*, the band spent five painstaking months recording and sequencing the album.

Ralph McTell had consistently provided precisely the material Fairport were looking for, and on their new album – 1995's *Jewel In The Crown* – they also found suitable material from Steve Tilston, Rob Beattie, Clive Gregson, Julie Matthews, and ... Leonard Cohen. The Cohen connection wasn't as incongruous as it seemed; circa 1968/69 Fairport used regularly to include poignant covers of Cohen's 'Bird On A Wire' and 'Suzanne' in their sets. And like Fairport, the gnomic bard had come a long way from the 1960s.

Reviewing *Jewel In The Crown* in *Q*, Mark Cooper noted: 'Their strengths here are Nicol's emergence as a vocalist of skill and a choice of songs that lean heavily on British songwriters like Steve Tilston, Jez Lowe and Clive Gregson, whose material sits comfortably alongside traditional ballads ... Modern-day Fairport are mostly good-natured, but there's no mistaking the venom in the opening title track, which gives British nationalism a good kicking.'

As well as delivering an album which could comfortably stack alongside Fairport's best-ever efforts, *Jewel In*

Epilogue, March 1997

The Crown also came – a Fairport first this – as a poppadom-shaped picture disc. This was a reference to the fact that the album's title wasn't just a sly dig at Empire-building, but also an homage to the band's favourite curry house in Banbury. In the competitive market place of 90s pop, a world of trip-hop and 12" white label dance remixes, a world where BBC Radio 1 refused to play a new single by The Beatles, Fairport Convention did well to sell 15,000 copies of *Jewel In The Crown*.

Casting their net wider, and in an ironic reversal, Fairport went unplugged for their next album, 1996's *Old, New, Borrowed, Blue*. It began life when the four-piece Fairport were forced to play minus drummer Dave Mattacks. ('I think he was fed up because nobody could be found to help him with his gear,' Simon Nicol offered as musical insight into the Unplugged experience.)

Close listening to Kate and Anna McGarrigle's debut album saw two tracks ('Foolish You' and 'Swimming Song') transferred to the Fairport acoustic album. 'The Hiring Fair' and 'Crazy Man Michael' were as seamless as ever, and Ric's fiddle lent spectral resonance. After all the care which had gone into *Jewel In The Crown*, it was no surprise that *Old, New, Borrowed, Blue* would be seen as little more than a pleasant souvenir of an interesting Fairport digression.

Onwards, ever onwards. Fairport entered 1997 once again locked firmly into anniversary mode. This was the big one: 30 years since that first gig at St Michael's Church Hall, Golders Green. There have been other bands who have kept going as long as Fairport (The Four Tops, Rolling Stones) and there have been bands that just seem to have been going as long as Fairport (Genesis, Aerosmith), but for a rock 'n' roll band to have kept solidly and persistently at it since 1967 is still worthy of close media attention.

The last time I went to see Fairport was at the Royal

Festival Hall on 2 February, 1997, the official London date to celebrate their 30th anniversary. It was a healthy crowd who flocked to the South Bank that Sunday night. Long-time fans couldn't help but reflect that it was on this very stage, 28 years before, that a younger and more nervous Fairport Convention had premiered their 'new direction', showcasing the *Liege & Lief* material.

As the only original member, the linking thread, I wondered what thoughts preoccupied Simon Nicol as he sang. 'Crazy Man Michael', 'Walk Awhile', 'Matty Groves', 'Meet On The Ledge', 'Who Knows Where The Time Goes' . . . these were songs inextricably linked to his past, the past of Fairport, and tied up too with the past of the loyal audience who are so closely bound with the band.

Ralph McTell performed solo as first-half closer, and a rewarding experience it was too. In the UK, Ralph seems destined to be identified either as composer of 'Streets Of London' – the one folk song well-known enough to get a quick laugh in a TV sketch – or as singer and composer of kiddies' songs. But that night it was his song about Derek Bentley, victim of a 1950s judicial murder, which made the strongest impact, and you were reminded too what a powerful acoustic guitarist Ralph still is.

The Festival Hall show was basically Cropredy with a roof on, but wherever they appear an enormous groundswell of goodwill greets Fairport. It has to do with communal memory, the power of songs to map out their listeners' lives, and not least, the conviviality of the chaps themselves. For the first time in a decade, Maartin Allcock was not there. ('It was musical differences,' Simon had explained helpfully beforehand. 'He was musical, we were different.') Maartin's place had been taken by old Fairport friend Chris Leslie, so there was a two-pronged vegetarian fiddle attack.

The '97 model Fairport is a vehicle for all-round entertainment. There are gags a-plenty, onstage business and showbiz routines. There is also, more remarkably, the ability to assimilate strong new material ('The Hiring Fair', 'Naked Highwayman', 'Jewel In The Crown') into a set already groaning with history.

There was something touching in seeing those distinguished gentlemen still drawing inspiration from the music which has already meant so much to so many. Accusations that Fairport are coasting on the easy victories of a comfortable past are best denied by seeing them in concert today.

Oasis or Mansun they are not. Nor were they ever meant to be. They are, quite simply, the greatest folk-rock band in the world today. They are, and remain, ladies and gentlemen, Fairport Convention.

So many journeys, so many miles travelled. All since that first gig in a London which still conducted its exchanges in pounds, shillings and pence. When Fairport began their career, The Beatles had barely released *Sgt Pepper* let alone *Anthology*. Jimmy Page was still in The Yardbirds, Jimi Hendrix was still on the planet and Elvis had not yet left the building.

'Who knows,' as the lady herself asked all those years ago, 'where the time goes?'

Patrick Humphries
London, March 1997

Discography by Ian Burgess

Albums

Year	Title	Label	Vinyl No.	CD No.
68	Fairport Convention (mono)	Polydor	582035	
68	Fairport Convention (stereo)	Polydor	583035	835230-2
	Fairport Convention (re-issue)	Polydor	2384 047	
69	What We Did On Our Holidays	Island	ILPS 9092	IMCD97
69	Unhalfbricking	Island	ILPS 9102	IMCD61
69	Liege & Lief	Island	ILPS 9115	CID9115
70	Full House	Island	ILPS 9130	
	Full House	Hannibal	HNBL4417	
	Full House	Carthage		CGCD 4417
71	Angel Delight	Island	ILPS 9162	IMCD166
71	Babbacombe Lee	Island	ILPS 9176	IMCD153
72	History of Fairport Convention	Island	FCD4	CIDD4
73	Rosie	Island	ILPS 9028	IMCD152
73	Nine	Island	ILPS 9246	IMCD154
74	Live Convention	Island	ILPS 9285	IMCD95
75	Rising For The Moon	Island	ILPS 9313	IMCD155
76	Gottle O' Geer	Island	ILPS 9389	
76	Live At The L.A. Troubadour	Island	HELP28	
77	Bonny Bunch Of Roses	Vertigo	9102 015	
	Bonny Bunch Of Roses (re-issue)	Woodworm	WR011	
78	Tipplers Tales	Vertigo	9102 022	
	Tipplers Tales	BGO	BGOLP72	BGOCD72

Discography

	Bonny Bunch Of Roses/Tipplers Tales	Vertigo		512 988-2
79	Farewell Farewell	Woodworm	BEAR22	
	Farewell Farewell	Simons	GAMA1	
	Farewell Farewell (w/extra track)	Road Goes On Forever		RGFCD001
	Farewell Farewell (w/extra track) Encore Encore	Terrapin Trucking		TRUCKCD 011
82	Moat On The Ledge	Woodworm	WR001	
85	Gladys' Leap	Woodworm	WR007	WRCD07
	Gladys' Leap	Terrapin		TRUCKCD
	Gladys' Leap (w/extra track)	Trucking		015
86	Expletive Delighted	Woodworm	WR009	WRCD09
	Expletive Delighted	Terrapin		TRUCKCD
	Expletive Delighted (w/extra track)	Trucking		016
87	In Real Time	Island	ILPS 9883	CID9883
87	House Full – Live In L.A. 1970	Hannibal	HNBL 1319	HNCD1329
87	Heyday: BBC Radio Sessions 68/69	Hannibal	HNBL 1329	HNCD1329
89	Red & Gold	New Routes	RUE002	RUECD002
	Red & Gold (re-issue)	Woodworm		WRCD019
	Red & Gold (w/extra track)	HTD		HTD CD 47
91	Five Seasons	New Routes	RUE005	RUECD005
	Five Seasons (re-issue)	Woodworm		WRCD020
	Five Seasons (w/extra track)	HTD		HTD CD 48
92	The Woodworm Years	Woodworm		WRCD015
	The Woodworm Years (w/extra tracks)	Silver Mist		SIV CD0005
92	25th Anniversary Pack	Island		FCBX1
93	25th Anniversary Concert	Woodworm		WRDCD022
95	Jewel In The Crown	Woodworm		WRCD023
97	Who Knows Where The Time Goes	Woodworm		WRCD025

Meet On The Ledge

FAIRPORT ACOUSTIC CONVENTION
96	Old New Borrowed Blue	Woodworm		WRCD024

DAVE PEGG
84	The Cocktail Cowboy Goes It Alone	Woodworm	WR003	WRCD020

SIMON NICOL
88	Before Your Time	Woodworm	WR010	WRCD010
	Before Your Time	Terrapin		TRUCKCD 017
	Before Your Time (w/extra track)	Trucking		
92	Consonant Please Carol	Woodworm		WRCD021

MAARTIN ALLCOCK
90	Maart	Woodworm		WRCD012

RIC SANDERS
84	Whenever	Waterfront	WF021	
	Whenever	Nico Polo		NP001
91	Neither Time Or Distance	Woodworm		WRCD017

SIMON NICOL AND DAVE SWARBRICK
82	Live At The White Bear	White Bear Records	WBR 001 S	
84	Close To The Wind	Woodworm	WR006	

DONALDSON/CLEYNDERT/MATTACKS
96	Sing The Line	Red Dot Records		RD00123

IMPORTANT OVERSEAS ALBUMS
76	Fairport Chronicles (USA)	A&M	SP-3530	
82	Folk With Poke (Australia)	Island	L37944	

Discography

NON-FAIRPORT ALBUMS INCLUDING EXCLUSIVE VERSIONS OF FAIRPORT SONGS:

SANDY DENNY
85	Who Knows Where The Time Goes	Island	SDSP100	
	Who Knows Where The Time Goes	Hannibal	HNBL 5301	HNCD5301

SANDY DENNY, TREVOR LUCAS & FRIENDS
96	The Attic Tracks 1972–1984	Special Delivery	SPDCD1052

RICHARD THOMPSON
76	Guitar, Vocal	Island	ICD8	
	Guitar, Vocal	Hannibal		HNCD4413
93	Watching The Dark	Hannibal		HNCD5303

ASHLEY HUTCHINGS
94	The Guv'nor Vol 1	HTD	HTDCD23
95	The Guv'nor Vol 2	HTD	HTDCD29
95	The Guv'nor Vol 3	HTD	HTDCD38
96	The Guv'nor Vol 4	HTD	HTDCD66

KIPPER FAMILY
86	The Crab Wars	Dambuster	DAM017

VARIOUS ARTISTS
86	Where Would You Rather Be Tonight	Sunrise	A40111M
75	The Electric Muse	Island/ Transatlantic	FOLK1001
88	Island Life	Island	IBX25

BERYL MARRIOTT (INC. SIMON NICOL, DAVE PEGG, DAVE MATTACKS, RIC SANDERS, MAARTIN ALLCOCK, CHRIS LESLIE)
91	Weave The Mirror	Woodworm	WRCD016

THE BUNCH (INC. SANDY DENNY, TREVOR LUCAS, DAVE MATTACKS, RICHARD THOMPSON, ASHLEY HUTCHINGS)
72	The Bunch	Island	ILPS9189

Meet On The Ledge

G.P.s (RICHARD THOMPSON, DAVE PEGG, DAVE MATTACKS, RALPH McTELL)

91	G.P.s		Woodworm		WRCD014
	G.P.'s		HTD		HTDCD53

Singles

67	If I Had A Ribbon Bow	If (Stomp)	Track	604020
69	Meet On The Ledge	Throwaway Street Puzzle	Island	WIP6047
69	Si Tu Dois Partir	Genesis Hall	Island	WIP6064
70	If (Stomp)	Chelsea Morning	Polydor	2058014
70	Now Be Thankful	Sir B. McKenzies...	Island	WIP6089
70	John Lee	The Time Is Near	Island	WIP6128
73	Rosie	Knights of the Road	Island	WIP6155
75	White Dress	Tears	Island	WIP6241
80	Rubber Band	Bonny Black Hare	Simons	PMW1
86	Quazi B. Goode		Sunrise	BONG 1
87	Meet On The Ledge	Si Beg Si Mor	Island	IS 324
87	Meet On The Ledge	Si Beg/John Barleycorn	Island	12IS324

AUSTRALIAN SINGLE WITH EXCLUSIVE TRACK

74	The Devil In The Kitchen	Possibly Parsons Green	Island	K5402

DAVE PEGG SINGLE

84	The Cocktail Cowboy	The Swirling Pit	Woodworm	WRS101

Videos

82	1980 Cropredy Re-Union 1982	Videotech	
82	Re-Union Festival Broughton Castle 1981	Videotech	VTV101

Discography

83	A Peculiar Old Weekend	Videotech VTV003
84	A Weekend In The Country	Videotech
86	Cropredy Capers (1986)	Intech
87	In Real Time	Island IVA001
87	It All Comes Round Again	Island IVA002
90	Live Legends (1990)	Castle Music Pictures CMP6013
91	Maidstone 1970	Musikfolk MF01
93	Live At Broughton Castle 15 August 1981	Musikfolk MF03
93	Alive In New York	Woodworm
95	Forever Young Cropredy 1982	Musikfolk MFV04

RIC SANDERS INSTRUCTIONAL VIDEO
Music Makers – The Violin   Virgin VVD915

Miscellaneous

OFFICIAL BOOTLEG TAPES
Airing Cupboard Tapes	(Various live sources)
AT2	(Cropredy 1982)
The Boot	(Cropredy 1993 double cassette)
The Other Boot	(Cropredy 1985 double cassette)
The Third Leg	(Cropredy 1987 double cassette)

FAN CLUB CASSETTES
86	Australia	Here Live Tonight	FOFC1	(Fairport)
86	Australia	More Live Tonight	FOFC2	(Fairport)
85	US	Doom And Gloom	FLYC001	(Richard Thompson Inc. Fairport Tracks)
91	US	Doom And Gloom Vol 2	FLYC003	(Richard Thompson Inc. Fairport Tracks)

Notes – Albums
The year quoted is that of the original release. The compact discs were released later in the case of earlier albums. The first simultaneous vinyl/cd release was *In Real Time*. *Live In L.A.* is partially the same as *Live At The L.A. Troubadour*, with some tracks omitted and others added. *Fairport Chronicles* is a collection album which includes Bunch and Sandy solo tracks. *Folk With Poke* is *Sloth* plus instrumentals; all tracks are

Meet On The Ledge

otherwise available. UK *History Of* ... cd omits two tracks from the original vinyl, both of which are on *Liege & Lief*. The Fairport 25th Pack included the *Babbacombe*, *Rosie*, *Nine*, *Rising* cds with no extra booklet or information of any kind. *Encore Encore* is a remastered, extended version of *Farewell Farewell* due for release in July 1997. *Gladys Leap*, *Expletive Delighted* and *Before Your Time*, all with extra tracks, are also due for release at the same time. At the time of writing no label/catalogue details have been allocated.

Notes – Singles
'Quazi B. Goode' features Jon Benns and Motorhead guitarist Wurzel. The B-side is 'Where Would You Rather Be Tonight?' by Mike Silver. The single was a charity release. The later release of 'Meet On The Ledge' is a re-recording by the 1987 line-up; the B-side track(s) are live recordings. Some copies of the 12" version included a family tree poster.

Ian Burgess who provided this discography runs *The Ledge*, which is the excellent UK Fairport fanzine.

Further details from Ian Burgess, 83 Windway Road, Llandaff, Cardiff CF5 1AH.

Cropredy Circles

Unfortunately there was not room this time round to include Pete Frame's beautifully drawn and informative family tree 'Resolving The Fairport Confusion'. However, it can be found, along with 29 others, in *The Complete Rock Family Trees* by Pete Frame (Omnibus Press, ISBN: 0-7119-0465-0).

Ashley Hutchings' Guv'nor releases are available from HTD Records, 1st Floor Suite, 159 Blendon Road, Bexley, Kent DA5 1BT.

Anyone wishing to find out what Ashley himself is planning for the future can find out by writing to Speaking Volumes, Huntingdon Hall, Crown Gate, Worcester WR1 3LD, UK. Fax: 01905 619958.

Porthole, a Fairport Convention quarterly, is published in the USA by Robert D. Lehrian, 212 Farmington Road, Pittsburgh, PA, 15215, USA.

Details of John Penhallow's Sandy and Trevor Attic Tapes can be obtained from PO Box 321, Alexandria, NSW 2015, Australia.

The years since the band's rebirth in 1982 have been thoroughly chronicled in *The Woodworm Era: The Story Of Today's Fairport Convention* by Fred Redwood & Martin Woodward (Jeneva Publishing, PO Box 5918, Thatcham, Berks RG18 9YY).

And for anyone who doesn't know, details of Fairport's Annual Cropredy Reunions can be obtained by writing to: PO Box 37, Banbury, Oxon OX16 8YN, UK.

List of Illustrations

SECTION I

Page 1
A very early Fairport gig, London, 1967. Left to right: Simon Nicol, Martin Lamble, Ashley Hutchings, Richard Thompson. Courtesy of Ashley Hutchings.

Later that same evening, Richard grows rock-star sunglasses. Courtesy of Ashley Hutchings.

The Fairport house and plaque. Neil Raphael and author's own collection.

Page 2
Fairport at the time of their first album. Left to right: Martin Lamble, Richard Thompson, Ashley Hutchings, Judy Dyble, Simon Nicol, Ian Matthews. Author's own collection (Ray Stevenson).

By the summer of 1968, Sandy Denny had replaced Judy Dyble. Courtesy of Island Records (Richard Bennett Zeff).

Page 3
Moody, Bergmanesque, and Ian Matthews gets the hat. Courtesy of Island Records (Richard Bennett Zeff).

Fairport get it together in the country, with assorted urchins, parkkeepers and Witchseason's Anthea Joseph between Martin and Simon. Courtesy of Ashley Hutchings.

Page 4
The crash, 12 May 1969, in which Martin Lamble and Richard's girlfriend, Jeannie Franklyn, lost their lives. Martin Lamble courtesy of Ashley Hutchings, remainder author's own collection.

Page 5
Later in 1969, Fairport hit *Top Of The Pops* with new boys Dave Swarbrick and Dave Mattacks. Courtesy of Island Records (Barry Plummer).

List of Illustrations

Pre-performance nerves backstage at the BBC. Left to right: Swarbrick, Thompson, Mattacks, Hutchings, Nicol, Denny. Courtesy of Ashley Hutchings (H. Goodwin).

Page 6
Fairport relax while creating *Liege & Lief* at Farley Chamberlayne, summer 1969. Courtesy of Island Records.

The Queen Anne mansion in Hampshire where the band lived while rehearsing. Courtesy of Ashley Hutchings.

Thompson swings! Courtesy of Ashley Hutchings.

Page 7
Full-page ad for the finished album, Melody Maker 6 December 1969. Author's own collection.

Page 8
The *Full House* line-up, 1970, after Sandy and Ashley split. Fresh-faced new bassist Dave Pegg between Richard and Swarbrick. Courtesy of Island Records.

The Angel, a converted pub which became Fairport's new home. Author's own collection.

Handbill from late 1970. Courtesy of Dave Burrows.

SECTION II

Page 1
Sandy post-Fairport at the time of *The North Star Grassman And The Ravens*. Courtesy of Island Records.

1971 Sandy gig, with a little help from Richard and Peggy. Courtesy of Island Records (Jay Myrdal).

Page 2
1884 account of 'The Murder of A Lady Near Torquay' that inspired Fairport's 1971 *Babbacombe Lee* album. Courtesy of Dave Pegg.

Page 3
Babbacombe Lee tour flyer from 1971. Courtesy of Dave Burrows.

LP inner sleeve. Author's own collection.

Stripped of all original members by departure of Simon and DM, Fairport's 1972 all-Brummie line-up. Left to right: Roger Hill, Tom Farnell, Swarbrick, Pegg. Courtesy of Island Records.

Page 4
Fairport's tenth line-up, responsible for *Rosie* and *Fairport 9*, introducing Jerry Donahue and Trevor Lucas. Courtesy of Island Records (Brian Cooke).

Meet On The Ledge

Recording at Sound Techniques Studio, 1974. Left to right: Pegg, Mattacks, Lucas, Donahue, Swarbrick. Courtesy of Dave Mattacks.

Page 5
Sandy rejoins Fairport to be with husband Trevor Lucas. Band photographed in St Peter's Square. Courtesy of Dave Pegg.
   On steps of Island Records, 1974. Courtesy of Island Records.

Page 6
Fairport enjoying life on the road, 1975. Courtesy of Island Records.
   Richard in the early days of Fairport. Courtesy of Island Records.
   Richard circa 1975, four years after quitting the band. Courtesy of Island Records.

Page 7
Fairport with goat, new drummer Bruce Rowland and – now you see him, now you don't – Simon Nicol. Courtesy of Dave Pegg.
   Hi-tech Fairport set list circa 1977 and souvenir beer mat. Courtesy of Dave Pegg.
   Fairport in 1976 pub horror shock drama! Left to right: Dan Ar Bras, Pegg, Swarbrick, Roger Burridge, Bruce Rowland, Bob Brady. Courtesy of Island Records.

Page 8
Fairport Split 1979. Definitely final-ever performance, last chance to see, never again, etc. Author's own collection.

SECTION III

Page 1
Gasp! Fairport back together again, rehearsals at Putney's Half Moon for first Cropredy reunion, 1980. Courtesy of Dave Pegg.
   Ticket for second reunion, held at Broughton Castle, 1981 – 'Bert Jansom', who he? Author's own collection.

Page 2
Richard Thompson, Judy Dyble and Ian Matthews. Courtesy of Ashley Hutchings.
   Dave Pegg. Courtesy of Island Records (Brian Cooke).

Page 3
Trevor Lucas, Dave Mattacks and Dave Swarbrick (Joseph Stevens). Courtesy of Island Records.
   Sandy Denny. Courtesy of Ashley Hutchings.

174

List of Illustrations

Page 4
Pegg and Mattacks at first rehearsal for *Galdys' Leap*, 1985. Courtesy of Dave Pegg (John Woodward).

Early days of the most enduring Fairport line-up, backstage at Cropredy 1986. Left to right: Mattacks, Maartin Allcock, Ric Sanders, Pegg, Nicol. Courtesy of Dave Pegg.

Page 5
Long-time Fairport colleague Ralph McTell, onstage at Cropredy. Courtesy of Dave Pegg (Lee Evans).

Aerial view of the festival site. Courtesy of Dave Pegg.

Band with Cynthia Payne, and (with luncheon vouchers) the legendary Johnny 'Jonah' Jones. Courtesy of Dave Pegg (Martyn Claydon).

Page 6
Ian Matthews joins Fairport onstage, Cropredy 1986. Courtesy of Dave Pegg (Tony Dyke).

All the young dudes? Pegg, Mattacks, Nicol, Thompson together again. Courtesy of Dave Pegg.

Page 7
Duelling fiddles, Ric Sanders and Swarbrick battle it out at Cropredy. Courtesy of Dave Pegg (Mark Dixon).

Two men, three guitars and not enough plectrums to go round! Courtesy of Dave Pegg (Johan Wingborg).

Page 8
Fairport 1997 on their 30th-anniversary tour. Courtesy of Ian Burgess.

Following the departure of Maartin Allcock, newcomer Chris Leslie completes the current Fairport Convention. Courtesy of Ian Burgess.

Current line-up. Courtesy of Dave Pegg (John Woodward).

Every attempt has been made to contact the copyright holders of material featured within this book. Any copyright holders of text or pictures inadvertently used without permission, please contact Virgin Publishing.

Thanks, 1997

Particular thanks to Ian Burgess for the Discography; and to Dave Burrows, Ashley Hutchings and Dave Pegg, for trawling the archives for Fairport photos.

Hannah MacDonald and Rebecca Levene at Virgin Books.

Susie Hudson at *Mojo*.

Stella and Cally (it all comes round again) at Island.

Sue Parr came into my life the year after *Meet On The Ledge* was published, and enjoys nothing more than spending every wedding anniversary at Cropredy.

Currently available on ![Island] Island Records

FAIRPORT CONVENTION
WHAT WE DID ON OUR HOLIDAYS

FAIRPORT CONVENTION
JOHN BABBACOMBE LEE

FAIRPORT CONVENTION
UNHALFBRICKING

FAIRPORT CONVENTION
ROSIE

FAIRPORT CONVENTION
LIEGE AND LIEF

FAIRPORT CONVENTION
THE HISTORY OF

FAIRPORT CONVENTION
9

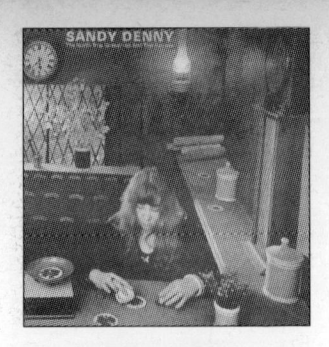

FAIRPORT CONVENTION
LIVE

FAIRPORT CONVENTION
RISING FOR THE MOON

FAIRPORT CONVENTION
IN REAL TIME

SANDY DENNY
THE NORTH STAR GRASSMAN AND THE RAVENS

SANDY DENNY
SANDY

SANDY DENNY
BEST OF

RICHARD & LINDA THOMPSON
I WANT TO SEE THE BRIGHT LIGHTS